Recipe for Romance

Maria Isabel Pita

an erotic romance

RECIPE FOR ROMANCE
Copyright ©2004 by Magic Carpet Books
All Rights Reserved

First Magic Carpet Inc. edition April 2004

Published in 2004

Manufactured in the United States of America
Published by Magic Carpet Books

Magic Carpet Books
PO Box 473
New Milford, CT 06776

Library of Congress Cataloging in Publication Date

Recipe For Romance by Maria Isabel Pita
ISBN 0-9726339-8-7

Book Design: P. Ruggieri

DEDICATION

In memory of my grandmother, Rosa Padron,
who never taught me how to cook
(I think I understand why now, abuelita)

And

In honor of my beautiful mother, Juana Rosa,
the poet who loves good food but prefers not to cook

AUTHOR'S NOTE

None of the feelings expressed in this book are fiction.

CHAPTER ONE

I realized what I had missed most about Miami was the sky. Up in Boston's North End, where I had lived for over five years the sky is often a deeply depressing grey trapped between stone buildings dark with age. I kept leaning over the black steering wheel of the burgundy Ford Contour I had rented at the airport, my snow-clouded vision hungrily drinking in the radiant south Florida sky... a sky the same clear blue color of my last boyfriend's eyes... but I definitely didn't want to think about him.

It was over between me and my most recent X (who seemed a real treasure at first, but who turned out to be no more than a very good imitation of a man) and ever since I had left him, I had experienced much more relief than sadness. For a briefly enjoyable time we had shared a passion for the outdoors, and climbed more than one mountain together; however, a hiking buddy is one thing, a husband is another, and ever since I was a little girl I had believed

I was destined to experience a love that would take me to unimagined heights inside…

I was still searching for that Mount Everest of passions, refusing to settle for anything less. I had come to prefer my own company to being with the wrong man, which I had discovered was infinitely worse than being alone. When you're by yourself at least you can be entirely yourself instead of struggling to fit into the often mysteriously cramped space of someone else's particular predilections and perceptions. The man I kept dreaming of would appreciate all of me, in every sense, I was sure of this; he would treasure every idiosyncrasy of my personality along with every unique curve of my flesh and I would never have to pretend with him about anything. In all my previous relationships with men I invariably compromised, restructuring my thoughts and feelings in little ways that did not seem significant in themselves, but after the inevitable breakup, when I added them all up, the result was always the same – a relationship and a routine at odds with my deepest being, which continued stubbornly expressing itself through dreams of true love. I had learned that being with the wrong man was like sitting down to a meal lacking in so many vital ingredients and spices that it was more frustrating for me than fulfilling.

I was fasting again, in between boyfriends, at ten o'clock in the morning driving down 37th Avenue in sunny south Florida. The city had changed a bit since I left it shortly after graduating from Florida International University with a Bachelor's degree in Fine Arts. Numerous tall condo buildings had sprung up on the highly coveted border between Miami (the poorest city in the nation) and Coral Gables, which costs as many dollars to live in as there are leaves on its beautiful old trees. I idly wondered exactly how much people were paying to live in those glorified beehives, most of them painted what was clearly one of the city's most popular legally approved pastel colors – a shade somewhere between yellow and orange. The new buildings had all grown quickly up out of the concrete, satisfying a growing demand for boring box-like homes that dreamed of being lusciously desirable tropical fruits worth sinking your financial teeth into.

Momentarily stopped at a traffic light, I flipped down the visor, slipped off my leopard-skin designer sunglasses, and quickly examined my face. It was mid-May and already stunningly hot outside. I had quickly switched on the engine and cranked up the air conditioner in the parking lot of the rental office, but the oven-like temperature inside the car when I got in had taken its toll on my make-up; my black eyeliner had pooled at the corners of my honey-brown eyes and my nose already needed another dusting of clear powder. The air conditioner's delicious arctic breeze caressed my shoulder-length hair, but just the short walk from the rental office to the car had aroused rebellious waves in its dark-brown fullness. I remembered one thing I didn't miss about Miami – the often one-hundred-percent humidity.

I plucked a tissue out of my black-leather purse, dabbed delicately at the corners of my eyes, thrust the tissue into my purse again, slipped my sunglasses back on, flipped the visor up, and accelerated beneath the green light. I knew exactly where I was going; I had attended more than one wake at this particular funeral home. This time it was my ninety-three-year-old grandfather's older sister who had passed away. My great aunt, Ana Maria Cabezon, had finally joined the angels with all her wits still in her possession at the remarkable age of one-hundred-and-two. She didn't leave a wheelchair behind, only the elegant cane she used to get around her little house, and to walk up and down Coral Way, where she did all her shopping and banking until the day of the night she went to sleep forever. To me my grandfather's sister had always been old and yet at the same time reassuringly eternal. Everyone in my family on my mother's side is long-lived. It's nice to know I possess such hearty Cuban genes, because apparently (I indulged in a rare moment of cynicism) it was going to take me a very long time to meet a man I could take seriously for more than a few months. I am blessed genetically, I exercise regularly although not excessively (in my opinion life is too short to waste going nowhere on cardio machines that are supposedly good for the heart and yet are dishearteningly boring, not to mention utterly deadening to the imagination) and one of my favorite pastimes is gourmet cooking married with nutritional awareness. Yet strangely enough, I had to teach myself how to cook; my timeless aunt never deigned to share any of her recipes with me – perhaps because she saw I was much more interested in mixing colors together with crayons, then with water colors and oil paints – and my mother only cooks out of necessity, resenting every moment she has to spend in the kitchen.

I could see right away that the small parking lot behind the funeral home was full of cars, but I miraculously managed to find a spot. I shut off the engine, dropped the rental key into my purse, and quickly opened the door, suddenly excited about seeing my family again, especially since I knew they couldn't be too annoyingly loud and boisterous inside a funeral home. One thing living up in Boston had done was reinforce my awareness, initially instilled in me by my soft-spoken American father, of just how loud Cubans can be when they get together. I imagined absolutely everyone I was related to would be at the wake – except dad, of course, whom mami had divorced years ago – and so would their friends and their friends, and so on. Cubans seem to love funerals almost as much as weddings. The deceased has just been welcomed into the Kingdom of Heaven (best-case scenario) shedding all the pains and tribulations of this earth, so the only thing to be sad about is how much you yourself (still stuck on this inferior side of reality) will miss them.

* * *

Gerald Evans watched the burgundy Contour make a sharp daredevil turn into the parking lot. Definitely a woman driver, he thought to himself, smiling as he squinted out at the rows of cars shining in the sunlight. He had just stepped outside for a moment to enjoy a refreshing breath of the hot, humid air that challenged his lungs almost like a mouthful of water and felt wonderful. He hated the artificial cold and shadow-draped stillness of the funeral home behind him.

He observed the door of the red Ford opening, and then a cool white high-heeled shoe stepping onto the burning-hot black asphalt. His squint deepened appreciatively as he followed the leg up, and up, to a black skirt enticingly cut at mid-thigh. Nice… Mm, very nice, he thought, thrusting his hands deep into the pockets of his black slacks as he watched the woman walking towards him. She appeared to be somewhere in her twenties, yet there was a mature gravity to her confident, unhurried stride that appealed to him. A classical nose held up a pair of leopard-handled sunglasses – two impenetrably dark pools above a mouth like a flower in full bloom. In his opinion, it took a truly beautiful woman to wear bright red lipstick without looking cheap, and this woman was beautiful, no doubt about that. Her dark hair, parted dramatically on one side, flowed down in a long, deep wave that nearly covered one of her eyes. Being a Film Noir movie buff, Gerald immediately compared her to a brunette Veronica Lake and, suddenly, he was in absolutely no hurry to leave the funeral home. He leaned back against the glass door and stepped back inside.

*   *   *

I saw the man in the black suit step back inside the building. He had been standing in front of the back door, tall and motionless as a shadow cast by a lamppost except for his visibly broad shoulders. I felt him watching me as I approached, but apparently he didn't find me very interesting since he didn't bother to wait for me to reach him before vanishing back inside, and his indifference made me somewhat cross.

For Christ's sake, Ariana, I thought, you're at a funeral home, not a night club! I seemed to be in the habit of mentally scolding myself lately. I hoped this meant I was developing an increasingly healthy objectivity towards my thoughts and feelings.

The white silk tank top I was wearing beneath a black cotton jacket was clinging to my perspiring skin by the time I made it into the building. In the dim light and chilly atmosphere, people walked across the plush carpet in front of me with the slow, silent grace of fish swimming deep underwater where the sun's light barely reaches. I shivered sensing a depth of grief surrounding me I knew could not possibly be coming from the room in which my aunt was lying; the almost palpable current of sorrow possessed an undertow of tragedy. It was flowing out from one of the other viewing rooms, and a quick glance in as I walked past told me it was full of young people. No wonder.

'It's Ani! Ani's here!' My mother's hushed cries steered me in the right direction.

'Hola, mami!' I had to bend over slightly to hug my blonde, reassuringly tender, mother. 'Ay, mami, it's so good to see you again!' I sighed. It had been too long since I experienced the sweet comfort of resting my head against the breasts that had suckled me nearly thirty years ago.

'Ani, mi amor, you look beautiful! Look, Elsa, Ariana's here!'

'My God, it can't be!' Elsa (my mother's best friend since childhood) exclaimed as quietly as she possibly could. 'Look at her! She looks so sophisticated!'

And so began the endless introductions and re-introductions in what for Cubans were painfully hushed voices. I had never been able to get all my relatives straight in my head, and I didn't bother trying to do so now. There were cousins and nieces and aunts and nephews, and great versions of all of those, plus a few great, great ones, and then there were the countless friends that went all the way back to the nineteen-thirties in Cuba, which practically made them family. There were so many people attending my great aunt's funeral that they were forced to mill out in the lobby and take turns paying their respects in the room where the body lay. It would have been impossible for me to actually greet everyone, and I somehow managed to reach my grandfather without being intercepted. He was attended by the court of his closest relatives, sitting enthroned in a chair beside the flower-bedecked casket.

'Abuelito,' I said tenderly, genuflecting beside him. As always, his thin, tall frame was impeccably dressed. When I was a little girl he always seemed like an old movie come to life to me; from the wide-brimmed black hat resting on his frail lap down to his silver-studded cane, he was the picture of elegance.

'Ay, Ani,' he sighed deeply, 'you have to have faith!' He lifted one of his arms and wrapped it briefly around me in a frail embrace. 'You just have to have faith, Ani,' he repeated, shaking his head sadly.

'I know, abuelito, I know.' I kissed his cool, paper-dry cheek tenderly. 'I'll be back,' I promised, and straightening up, I crossed my hands over my womb and went to stand over the casket for a respectful moment. I was glad it was closed; I would much rather remember my great aunt gesturing passionately with her hands, her black eyes glowing with memories as she told one of her endless stories. If I could believe them, I was descended from fascinatingly eccentric people. My favorite tale was the one about my three great-great green-eyed aunts. Apparently, they were so beautiful that men stopped dead on the street when they walked by. They were also very rich, and not one of them ever married, ironically afraid men only wanted them for their money. When one of them went to see a gynecologist as an old woman, the doctor shook his head and remarked, 'What a waste!' when he realized she was still a virgin.

Aware that almost all the eyes in the room were on me, I crossed myself, then turned and walked with the slow elegance of a model down a runway of admiring relatives. My mother, Rosa, was still standing near the entrance of the room, engaged now in a quietly intense conversation with Ernesto, an editor for El Nuevo Herald.

'Hola, Ernesto,' I said, smiling.

'Ani!' He smiled at me warmly; he and my mother had known each other since I was a little girl. 'How are you, young lady? You look stunning.'

'I'm great, thank you,' I replied somewhat truthfully, and bent to whisper in Rosa's ear, 'I'm going to grab a coffee, mami, but I'll be right back.'

Her amber-colored eyes widened in disbelief. 'You haven't had any coffee yet today?'

'Just a little on the plane from Boston.'

'Oh, please!' She shooed away the disgusting thought. 'That

dirty water they call coffee? Go have some real coffee and then hurry back. Everyone's dying to talk to you.'

'I know.' They all wanted to grill me about my love life to determine if there was a potential husband on the horizon.

Firmly clutching my purse like my independence, I hurried across the plant-filled lobby. A faint throbbing in my temples was threatening to become a pounding headache if I didn't get some caffeine into me soon, and maybe something else I loved dearly – Cuban toast. There was nothing like Cuban bread up North, a bread so light and fluffy it possesses an almost cracker-like texture when flattened in a sandwich grill, and the taste is heaven when it's brushed with hot butter. I love to cook, but I am an absolutely terrible baker, so I had mami ship some Cuban bread up to me in Boston, where the long loaves take up most of my chest freezer. Plenty of freezer space is essential when you love to eat well absolutely every night and you can't afford to eat out at restaurants all the time.

I had almost made it to the little coffee shop at the back of the building when an arm in a black suit suddenly barred my way in. 'Allow me,' said a deep, quiet voice.

I glanced up, and met intensely dark-grey eyes. 'Thank you...' I felt breathlessly caught by the black holes of his pupils... they seemed to be mysteriously pulling me into them, crushing my ability to think straight...

He smiled. 'My pleasure.'

Despite the fact that he was invading my personal space by standing so close, I had absolutely no desire to escape the warm gravity of his body as I walked ahead of him into the narrow coffee shop. It was empty except for an old man standing behind the counter wearing a white apron beneath a profoundly indifferent expression. I set my purse down on the counter, and perched carefully on one of the stools. I didn't have to look at the man seating himself beside me to be aware of the fact that he had noticed the way my skirt hiked up my thighs when I sat down. Shyly pleased by his attention, I sat up straight and crossed my bare legs (I would not even consider wearing pantyhose in such a hot climate.)

'What are you in the mood for?' the stranger asked me, and the pitch of his voice vibrated across my nerve-endings in a strangely wonderful way.

I hooked one of my high-heels into the metal support bar running the length of the counter to brace myself as I glanced at him. His brown hair was cut so short I wondered if he was in the military, but I immediately dismissed the possibility; the way he was leaning against the counter was much too sensually relaxed for a soldier. By way of reply, I said to the waiter, 'Un café con leche y una tostada, porfavor.'

'And a cortadito for me, please.'

The old man blinked as he absorbed our orders, then turned slowly around to begin filling them.

'We're going to be here a while,' the handsome stranger remarked, the trace of a smile still warming his lips.

It pleased me he sounded more amused than impatient. 'Yes,' I agreed, primly clasping my hands on the counter not knowing what else to do with them. I was just a little annoyed by how strangely awkward this man was making me feel. I had dated a considerable number of attractive men in my life, so I couldn't quite understand why this one in particular was having such a profound effect on my physical coordination.

'Aren't you going to tell me your name?' he asked when I glanced at him again.

'Ariana Padron,' I replied, no longer resisting the desire to look straight at him.

He held out his right hand. 'Gerald Loren.'

I realized my own hands were clenched when I had to pry them apart in order to return his firm grasp. I have always felt you can tell a lot about a person from their handshake, and I approved of his so much my heart started beating faster. In that instant I noticed that his slender upper lip rested over a slightly more tender lower lip, and they were both surrounded by a five o'clock shadow which struck me as sensually deliberate; the exciting ghost of a goatee taking form around his firm mouth made his smile seem even softer somehow.

'So,' he turned slightly on his stool to lean back against the wall facing me, 'who died?'

The offhand way he asked such a momentous question made me snap, 'You obviously didn't lose anyone near and dear to you.'

'I'm sorry.' He turned towards the counter again abruptly. 'I didn't mean to sound flippant; it's my defense mechanism against things I don't feel like dealing with.' His profile took on a serious cast that made him even more strikingly attractive. 'I'm working on it,' he added, givng me a rueful, sideways smile.

I immediately regretted my sharp tone. 'My great aunt passed away,' I informed him in a mild, forgiving voice. 'She was one-hundred-and-two.'

'Wow.' He glanced up at the ceiling as though trying to see through it and catch a glimpse of the old woman's incredibly resilient spirit. 'Cubans seem to live an amazingly long time,' he observed, studying me soberly.

'Some of them do, maybe too long. Why are you here?'

'The sister of a friend of mine was killed in a car accident.' He turned his head to watch the old man's ritually slow movements. 'She was only eighteen.'

'My God!' I exclaimed. 'The poor thing.'

He glanced down at the dull white counter. 'Yeah.'

'What a waste,' I added sadly.

He looked back at my face again firmly, 'All the more reason for those of us who still have a chance not to blow it,' he said.

'Amen.'

He held my eyes. 'Then what time should I pick you up?'

'Excuse me?' I was sure I hadn't heard him correctly.

'We should celebrate life and death the proper way,' he explained, 'like the ancient Egyptians used to do, with feasting and dancing, and everything else that makes like worth living.'

I looked away. 'Everything else?' I asked pointedly.

'A walk on the beach in the moonlight; a good movie; listening to music; a glass of wine and a gourmet meal... I would be honored if you would share any or all of the above pleasures with me, Ariana Padron.'

I met his eyes again. 'Well, when you put it that way, how can I possibly refuse?'

'You can't.'

His regard was so penetratingly direct, I suddenly felt breathless again. 'Yes I can,' I forced myself to correct him, tossing my hair away from my face defiantly, 'I just don't want to refuse.'

'Of course you don't.' He smiled. 'Why refuse what you want?'

'Sometimes you have to,' I said quietly, thinking of my blue-eyed ex-boyfriend.

'Then it's not really what you want,' he stated with conviction. 'Sometimes you think you want something because you're afraid of something else, which is what you really want.'

'What do you mean? Afraid of what?'

He shrugged. 'All sorts of things. Gracias,' he said to the old man as he brought over our coffees.

I was grateful for something to do with my hands. 'I'm sorry, but I don't think I know what we're talking about anymore, Gerald.' I decided I liked the feel of his name on my tongue.

He stared down at his already empty little cup as he twirled it around and around. 'I think you do,' he insisted quietly.

Strangely enough I realized he was right, and the stab of excitement I experienced warned me this man was dangerous. 'Are you a psychiatrist?' I demanded politely, instinctively searching for a weapon with which to defend myself against him.

His laugh was a deep, almost silent tremor in his chest reminiscent of a large cat's purr. 'No, I'm not,' he smiled at me again, 'but thanks for asking.'

I smiled back at him until my tostada suddenly arrived, then I eyed the long, butter-soaked slices of grilled Cuban bread in dismay. Not only was I suddenly not hungry, I couldn't imagine casually chewing and swallowing anything with this man watching me.

'I'll bet you normally take your butter on the side,' he teased.

'Yes, but they don't have tostadas up in Boston, so I thought I'd splurge.'

'Boston?'

'That's where I live.' I sipped my deliciously sweet hot coffee.

His cup chimed against the saucer as he turned it upside down, and pushed it away from him in a 'Well, so much for that' sort of gesture.

'I flew down for the funeral.' I cruelly turned the knife, immensely pleased by his reaction.

'I see.' He reached into a back pocket of his slacks for his wallet. He had long, strong legs to match his broad shoulders; his suit draped over him beautifully. 'How long will you be in Miami?' He merely sounded polite now.

'I don't know.' There was a roundtrip ticket in my purse, but I suddenly heard myself say, 'I keep thinking about moving back down.'

He tossed a five-dollar bill onto the counter, then thrust his wallet back into his pocket, and I was torn between another enticing view of his tight ass and the adorable dimple suddenly digging deep into his right cheek as he smiled up at the calendar hanging on the wall across from us. 'It's the first Friday of the month,' he announced.

'So it is.' I entertained the strange thought that if his head was dipped in a vat of plaster his profile would come out looking very much like an ancient Roman bust.

'Do you like art?' he asked as though reading my mind.

'I love art; it's one of life's greatest pleasures.'

'Then meet me at the America's Collection gallery on the corner of Ponce de Leon and Andalucia at eight o'clock this evening. We'll check out the new exhibits before dinner.'

I mimicked his matter-of-fact tone, 'Okay, I'll see you there.'

He got up to leave, but then paused just behind my stool. 'Are you staying with your family, Ariana?' He was standing so close to me his black jacket seemed to merge with mine, and I had to turn my head to look up at him.

'Yes, with my mom.'

He rested his hand lightly on my shoulder for an instant. 'I'll see you tonight,' he promised quietly.

The warmth of his touch lingered long after he left, seeping into my muscle through my jacket and mysteriously relaxing me, yet at the same time excitement painfully mingled with anxiety began gnawing at my stomach. I pushed my tostada away. It was too soon; I had just broken up with someone. And yet I didn't have a choice, I had to see this man again; he was as impossible to resist as the law of gravity. I was falling for him fast, and I was honest enough with myself to admit there was absolutely nothing I could do about it. Already the fear he might not show up at the gallery tonight was destroying my peace of mind. He hadn't asked for my phone number, which either meant he was infinitely confident or he didn't much care whether I showed up or not.

'Oh, God,' I said, shoving my hair away from my face. 'What am I getting myself into now?'

The old man stared tactfully into space.

CHAPTER TWO

It was after four o'clock in the afternoon when I finally returned to the steaming-hot shell of my rental car. The long day stretched behind me in a black-and-white blur of powder-coated old women dressed in black dresses; black limousines with bone-colored leather interiors; motorcycle cops in black-leather boots and tight black pants, their white helmets shining beneath the brutal sun as they parted traffic for the funeral procession on the way to the cemetery; and finally there was the dark earth waiting to receive my great aunt surrounded by white lilies. Afterwards, walking into the popular Cuban restaurant Versailles, with all its mirrors reflecting colorfully dressed patrons cheerfully laughing and talking, proved a stimulating contrast. It was time to stop feeling sad and to celebrate Ana Maria's ascent into Paradise. Cubans don't tend to feel guilty about the fact that death sharpens the appetites of those left behind, and true to this half of my nature, I indulged in one of my favorite dishes, Cuban Chicken Fricassee. I had struggled to re-create the recipe until my taste-buds at last told me it was just like I remembered it tasting when I was a little girl and every mouthful was an innocent orgasm. It came served with White Rice.

CUBAN CHICKEN FRICASSEE

Fortunately, either bottled or canned Sofrito – the basic backbone of many Caribbean and Spanish recipes consisting of olive oil, onions, garlic, green peppers and tomatoes simmered into a richly flavorful sauce – is now available in almost all major grocery stores. Naturally, you can make Sofrito from scratch yourself, but one of my personal Cooking Commandments is I shall spend as little time as possible slaving in the kitchen while preparing delicious meals. If I am going to be chained to anything it's to my bed by a deliciously handsome man, not to the stove.

Absolutely do not substitute skinless chicken thighs; I tried that once in a guilty effort to cut fat and, trust me, it doesn't work. This is a dish to be relished when you're in the mood for some passionate comfort food.

10 -12 skin-on Chicken Thighs
One Lemon
Salt (I recommend iodized Sea Salt)
Freshly ground Black Pepper
Minced Garlic (the kind that comes packed in a jar with olive oil works just fine)
Extra Virgin Olive Oil

1 16 oz can or bottle of Sofrito
2 Cans sliced (cooked) Potatoes (drained and well rinsed)
1 Bay Leaf
1/2 cup White Wine (NOT White Zinfandel, please!)
Pinch of Sugar (unrefined is best)
Pinch of Paprika
1 1/2 cups pimento-stuffed Green Olives, chopped

Season the skin-on chicken thighs with the fresh Lemon Juice, lots of Salt and freshly ground Black Pepper, and a generous amount of minced Garlic, then marinate them for one or two hours in the refrigerator.

In a very large deep-sided pan, pour enough Olive Oil to cover, heat on high, then add the Chicken Thighs, reserving the Marinade. Fry on both sides until nicely browned.

Pour the White Wine over the chicken, and let it burn away for a minute or two before adding the Marinade and the remaining ingredients, sprinkling a little additional Salt and pepper over the sliced Potatoes.

Bring to a boil, stirring to combine, then reduce the heat to medium-low, cover, and simmer – turning the thighs and stirring the mixture every half-hour or so – until the sauce begins to thicken. Fricassee is like Chili in that the longer it simmers the better it tastes. You don't want the sauce to be too thin, but you don't want it to be too thick, either. During the last half-hour or so of cooking, uncover the pan, turn the heat up to medium-high, and boil until the sauce is just the right consistency.

This recipe is designed for leftovers. You'll want leftovers! What you don't eat will freeze very nicely, just never defrost it or re-heat it in a microwave. Defrost the leftovers overnight in the refrigerator, and reheat them in the oven covered with tinfoil until hot.

Serve with White Rice.

PERFECT WHITE RICE

2 Cups Water
A generous dash of Canola Oil
1 generous tsp Sea Salt
1 Cup Long-Grain White Rice

Combine the first three ingredients in a small saucepan (if it's too large the rice will stick to the bottom and burn) and bring almost to a boil before adding the Rice. Stir well, cover and bring to a full rolling boil before turning the heat down as low as possible. Cook for an hour, then stir, continuing to cook over extremely low heat until all the moisture is absorbed.

* * *

My belly pleasantly full after the delicious Cuban feast at Versailles, I groaned in the grip of the sweltering humidity trapped inside my car, and yet, paradoxically, I was looking forward to getting home to my mami's house and taking a long hot shower.

I thrust the key into the ignition, turned it, then stared down in disbelief at the fragment of metal resting in my hand – the key had snapped neatly in half. Part of it was stuck in the ignition, the other part was in my hand. Well, at least the engine was purring quietly, which meant I wasn't stuck in the parking lot of a funeral home.

I promptly switched on the air conditioner; I couldn't possibly think straight with the skin melting over my bones.

'Why me?' I groaned, angrily shifting into reverse, then rocketing out of the parking spot only to have to wait impatiently for my chance to turn left onto 37th Avenue. The last thing I felt like doing was driving back to the rental office for a new car. This one still worked just fine, and it even seemed oddly special to me now... I couldn't help feeling it was meaningfully symbolic I was suddenly in possession of the two halves of a broken key that had to be joined to become whole, and of course I felt this way because of the mysteriously handsome stranger I had met this morning in the funeral home. A broken car key was an annoying problem, yet I couldn't help smiling. I am both intensely positive and somewhat overly dramatic by nature, so even the smallest details often strike me as profoundly significant. I essentially believe all the events in my life form the pieces of a cosmic puzzle...

I was tempted to drive to mami's and deal with the problem of the broken key tomorrow, but that was out of the question since there was no guarantee I could get the car started again. If memory served me correctly, there had to be at least one or two locksmiths on Coral Way who could extract the half of the key stuck in the ignition and make a whole new copy for me. It would be faster than driving back to the airport for another car; therefore, I determinedly turned left onto 22nd and began scanning both sides of the street for the type of business I needed. The big old trees growing on the islands dividing the road made it a bit difficult to see, but it wasn't long before I spotted what I was looking for on my left.

I made an illegal U-turn, and pulled into a parking spot along the curve. It wasn't yet five o'clock; the place should still be open and I might still be able to enjoy a long hot shower, and maybe even a little cat-nap, before getting ready for my date with Gerald.

Holding my breath, I inserted my half of the key into the ignition and quickly flicked my wrist. It worked; the engine shut off.

I slipped out of the car careful to leave it unlocked, slipped three quarters into the rusty old parking meter, and pulled open the heavy glass door leading into the locksmith's shop.

I was relieved to see there weren't any other customers in the store as I stepped up to a glass counter. Behind it stretched rows of work tables littered with fragments of metal, and cluttered with all sorts of arcane equipment for cutting, grinding, smoothing, and whatever else the marriage of locks and keys requires. There wasn't a soul in sight.

'Hola?' I called hopefully.

Silence.

'Hello?' I repeated impatiently.

Directly across from me at the back of the store a door opened, and a man dressed in tight black jeans and a short-sleeved black T-shirt stepped purposefully into the room looking down at something he was holding in his hands. He didn't seem to see me as he stopped at one of the worktables and switched on one of his many power tools. Apparently, he hadn't responded to my call and I didn't say anything because I was too busy staring at him in disbelief. Since when did locksmiths look like that?

I had recently been to an exhibit at the Museum of Fine Arts up in Boston entitled The Vikings. Apparently, these Scandinavians had been in the habit of hoarding scraps of silver and stashing them away in secret places where only they could find them (if they survived, that is, which many of them obviously didn't) and now staring at the man bending over a table of metal fragments, I felt as though I had come upon a hidden treasure myself. It didn't seem possible you could find a handsome Norseman in a dusty old shop in South Florida, but there he was, and the broken key in my hand had led me straight to him.

I cleared my throat. 'Um, excuse me...'

'I'll be with you in a second,' he replied without looking up.

I shifted impatiently onto one high-heeled foot. My shoes were killing me, and I had been wearing the same clothes for much too long, since four o'clock that morning, to be precise. They felt uncomfortably heavy with all the different atmospheres their silk and cotton molecules had absorbed today – Boston's melancholy mist, the airplane's stale dry air, the funeral home's chilly purity, the restaurant's rich smells, not to mention the rental car's hot oven – and I was dying to peel them off so my thoughts and feelings could flow comfortably together for a while in a long hot shower.

The high-pitched grinding of the electric saw the Miami Viking was using made me grit my teeth, and then the deep silence that followed the grating noise made me feel as though I was being deliberately ignored. 'Excuse me,' I repeated, shifting onto my other heel indignantly, 'but I'm kind of in a hurry...'

He finally glanced at me. 'I'm almost... done.'

Our eyes locked across the room, and I held my breath as though suddenly plunged into crystal-clear water alive with dangerous, hard-to-resist currents.

He literally dropped what he was doing and walked towards me slowly as though intentionally letting me get a good look at him. His jeans were so tight I wondered if they were even safe for him to wear, but I was glad he had risked it.

'What can I do for you?' he asked. He didn't smile, as though the question was intensely serious.

I held out my hand. 'The other half of the key is stuck in the ignition of my rental car outside,' I explained, indicating the street with a toss of my head which also served to get the hair out of my eye.

'Hmm, that's too bad.'

My indignation slipped and faltered on his perfect bone structure, then seemed to burn away in the reddish-blond hair combed neatly back away from his face. 'That's too bad?' I repeated, urging him to explain what exactly he meant by that so I wouldn't be forced to get angry with him.

'It's too bad the guy who owns this place is gone for the day. I'm just helping him out for a few weeks, and learning as I go.'

'So you can't help me?' I couldn't believe it; this man looked like he could do anything he wanted to.

'I didn't say that,' he replied coolly. 'Can you start the car up again?'

'Yes, I think so.'

'Then bring it around back and I'll see what I can do.'

* * *

Both front doors of the burgundy Ford were wide open and I was bent over on the passenger side looking into the car. The Viking lay sprawled across the front seat on his back, one of his legs braced on the door beside me, the other leg bent up into a black pyramid in front of me. His head was flung back beneath the steering wheel, exposing the vulnerable white slope of his neck. I was intently watching the muscles in his muscular upper arms tense as he determinedly jiggled a needle-fine instrument deep into a mysterious crack between the ignition and some other mechanical organ I didn't know the name of. I hadn't really listened to the explanation he gave me for what he was doing; I was too busy enjoying the view.

We were alone in a little private lot behind the store surrounded by concrete walls. It was late in the day, but the sun was still a long way from setting. It was hot in the car and I could tell he was sweating; the pale skin of his arms shone like marble.

'How can you still be so white living in Miami?' I asked curiously. I also felt compelled to try and entertain him. He had been operating on my car for over fifteen minutes now – a grueling, boring task – and the least I could do was make conversation.

'I have no idea.' Despite his awkward position he still managed to shrug.

My eyes kept gravitating to the dark space between his thighs. The longer he lay there like that, the harder it was to tell my hands they couldn't obey the electrical impulses my brain was sending them to explore… 'You must wear sun block,' I insisted in an effort to distract myself.

'SPF 32,' he confirmed. 'I don't much relish the thought of skin cancer. Unfortunately, I usually forget to put it on.'

I laughed, relieving some of my pleasantly growing tension. I didn't want to be late for my date with Gerald, but I was in no hurry to escape the company of this hardworking Norseman. 'Is there any hope?' I asked.

'There's always hope.'

I liked his response. 'Is it going to take much longer?'

'I don't know since I really don't have any idea what I'm doing.'

I almost slapped his thigh playfully… hungrily. 'Then maybe you should just give up,' I suggested reluctantly.

'I never give up, baby.'

I straightened up to take a deep, sobering breath of the refreshingly cool evening air. I was going to be a lovely night for a walk around the galleries, and I felt intensely alive, maybe because I had been at a funeral today… or maybe because I had flirted with two very attractive men today. Yet 'flirting' wasn't the word to describe what I had experienced with Gerald. I was enjoying myself at the moment, but I was in complete control, merely making the best of a little technical glitch in my day. I was having a little fun, but soon, with either half a key or a whole one, I was driving away; end of story.

I bent over into the car again just in time to see him shift his lean hips and strain his whole body in an effort to thrust deeper into my ignition. It was such an exciting sight, I found myself wondering what I would say if he asked me out. I would be tempted to accept, but I would also, I realized, easily be able to refuse. When Gerald essentially commanded me to meet him at the gallery, I felt a profound relief I would be seeing him again and knew I would have done almost anything to keep him in my orbit.

'What's your name?' I asked this other man abruptly.

'Eric McGregor. Thanks for caring.'

'You're Irish?'

'Yes, but long since exiled to the lovely swamps of Westchester. My father's family is from Ireland, my mother's from Venezuela.'

'Then you speak Spanish?'

'Don't sound so amazed.'

'I'm sorry, it's just that you look just like a Viking.'

'I'll take that as a compliment. So what's your name, beautiful?'

'Ariana Padron, half Cuban, half American on my dad's side.'

'And what do you do for a living, Ariana?'

'I'm a freelance writer and editor.'

'Sounds interesting. What's your work like?'

'It varies. I'm a freelancer. At the moment, I'm writing life-style articles for a variety of e-zines, including some pieces on food and nutrition. Trite as it may sound I'm seriously working on a cook book.'

'Really? I'd love to read your articles and taste your recipes. I love a woman who's into her career, but also has time for the sadly endangered domestic arts. Anyway, I think…' His arms flexed beautifully. 'I think I've got it!' He sat up so abruptly I didn't have time to get out of his way. His eyes were suddenly so close they drowned my awareness of everything else, and I couldn't see any reason not to let his mouth lightly touch mine for an instant. His lips were cool and firm, and far as my pulse was concerned a complete flat-line; I didn't feel anything except the pleasant, gentle sensation. Nevertheless, I was a bit flustered as I backed out of the car, and straightened up. I smoothed my hair away from my face. It was slightly damp at the temples, and my silk shirt was sticking to my back, yet I realized the cotton panties beneath my skirt were surprisingly dry.

Following me lithely out of the car, he tossed his half of the key triumphantly into the air. 'Not bad,' he declared, trapping the fragment of metal in his fist as it fell, 'for a cop.'

'You're a policeman?' I asked breathlessly. I couldn't help it; it turned me on that he had the right to restrain me if I decided to be a bad girl…

He slammed the car door closed behind him. 'I'm suspended from active duty at the moment, that's why I'm helping my friend out here for a few weeks.' He strode around the hood. 'I've got nothing better to do,' he closed the door on the driver's side, 'and I need the money.'

I had to admire his frankness. 'Why were you suspended?'

'Not for kissing women without their permission, if that's what you're thinking. Come on, let's go inside and I'll make you a shiny new key.'

I retrieved my purse from the top of the car, and followed him into the narrow little corridor at the back of the shop, where he abruptly stopped and turned sideways so I could walk in ahead of him. The belated gentlemanly gesture was a double-edged sword since I was forced to brush up against him on my way in. I experienced a faint lightning flash of heat in my belly as my soft breasts brushed his hard chest, but my heart handled his smile as easily as I had once played jump rope. He was just a bit too muscular, just a bit too obvious, but I was having fun, and I stood closer to him than I should have while he pieced my key together, made a mold of it, and forged a new one.

'There you go.' He held it up between us.

Respecting the spirit of the game, I reached for it.

He let me take it, but then swift as a snake striking, he caught my hand in his.

'How much do I owe you?' I asked, able to wrest my hand free only because he let me, making a point about his superior strength, and it excited me against my will.

'You owe me a drink,' he said. 'I'm about to close up.'

'Can you take a rain check? I just flew into town this morning for my great aunt's funeral and it's been a long day.'

'I'm sorry. Where are you staying?'

'With my mom. She has a house in the Gables.'

'Nice. Then how about meeting me for a drink tomorrow night? I'm warning you, if you try to say "no" I'll just have to find an excuse to arrest you. I was forced to give up my gun, but I still have my handcuffs.' With the back of his hand he gently lifted a glossy dark wing of hair out of my eye. 'Be a good girl, Ariana,' he urged quietly, his fingertips stroking my cheek as he let his hand fall, 'and say "yes".'

'I'm not a girl anymore.' Considering how the rest of me responded to his sexy threat, I was very pleased with my cool reply.

'Good, because I much prefer women, girls are too easy, yet at the same time they're almost impossible to please.' As he spoke, he walked to the front of the shop and locked the door. 'Anything turns them on,' he added, turning the sign so the side that said Closed faced the street, 'but they don't know their bodies well enough yet to experience truly intense pleasure the way a woman can.' He returned to stand directly in front of me.

I was more impressed by his perceptions than shocked by how intimate our conversation had become.

'You have to let me buy you a drink, Ariana,' he insisted.

'Well…' I had no idea what was going to happen with Gerald tonight, and it had been a long day; I didn't have the strength to resist, but I also didn't need to surrender completely. 'Give me your number and I'll call you, Eric. Maybe I can fit you in…'

His eyes narrowed as though my tone had made him catch sight of a dangerous possibility. 'Why not fit me in right here and now, Ariana?' he asked so quietly it was almost possible for me to believe I had only imagined the proposition. I have no idea why I hesitated to respond; I should have said 'No' at once and turned my back on him for daring to insult me like that, but for some reason I just stood there letting him hold my eyes long enough for him to reasonably interpret my silence as submission. Even when he took the key out of my hand again and laid its pristine metal body on the counter, I had time to protest, yet I remained as silent as my great aunt lying on her eternal silk bed deep in the earth. I was hypnotized by this strikingly handsome man's confidence and directness; there was something irresistibly pure about his maleness that was already intoxicatingly mixed in my imagination with authority and forcefulness.

'Come on,' he whispered, gently taking my hand as though he realized I was under a spell that could easily be dispelled if his attitude was not appropriately reverent. He led me to the back of the shop, and opened the door to a room that had to be windowless because it was pitch-black… black as the pupils in Gerald's eyes as he held the coffee shop door open for me… black as the suit Gerald was wearing… In my oddly compliant state, I scarcely realized I was thinking about one man while docilely following another one into the small lunch room that was revealed by the dim overhead light he flicked on. I took in a small wooden table and two chairs, a shelf holding an ancient microwave, a coffee maker accompanied by the usual entourage of Styrofoam cups, plastic spoons and refined sugar, and a tiny refrigerator purring quietly in a corner. The walls were bare, and the dark-gray floor was concrete; I could feel its chill through my high-heels, and for some inexplicable reason its cold hardness turned me on. The down-to-earth, bare-bones atmosphere of that bleak little room acted like a perverse aphrodisiac on my senses as Eric closed the door by turning to face me, and pressing me up against it, letting me feel the hard bulge growing inside his tight jeans. He was so tall his buried erection pressed into the base of my belly, making me thrillingly conscious of my bikini panties pressed damply against my labial lips and affording me no real protection whatsoever. I caught my breath in disbelief that I was about to let a complete stranger's cock-head kiss my sex lips and then thrust casually up between them, but it was definitely going to happen; already one of his hands had slipped between my legs and up my skirt while his other hand flung open my jacket and covered one of my breasts through the silk top.

'Mm…' he said. His clear blue eyes burned into mine like ice as he yanked my cotton panties down with one hand just far enough to cup my pussy possessively, and he smiled almost grimly as I gasped from the pleasurable shock.

'I – I've never done anything like this before,' I confessed.

'Are you afraid?' he asked quietly, his smile dimming as his thumb searched for my clitoris amidst the slick folds of my smoothly shaved sex lips.

'No,' I whispered truthfully.

'Why, because I told you I was a cop?' His thumb found my sensitive little button, and began undoing me from the inside out by gently circling and teasing, so that there was no way I could even think of resisting what was happening now.

'No...' I loved the way his other hand kneaded my breast through my shirt, breathlessly arousing me with the sensation of my stiff nipple pressed against his even harder palm.

'I want to get naked with you, Ariana. I want to take my time with you.' Despite the tender promise, his voice was rough. 'But not now... right now I'm just going to turn you around and fuck you.'

I remained submissively silent as my eyes silently commanded him not to disappoint me. A collage of images and feelings accumulated throughout the eventful day darkened my mind, stoking my sexual excitement in a haunting way, and all I wanted in those illicit moments outside time was the ultimate experience of a big, hard cock filling me up. I didn't need to see it to know this man possessed a hard-on that could stab all the thoughts out of me. As he stepped back to unzip his jeans, I quickly turned around and braced myself on the door with both hands, pushing my hips invitingly back towards him. I didn't even want to see his penis; all I wanted was to blindly, wantonly experience its thrusts not knowing anything about it just as I scarcely knew anything about the man behind it... the man wielding his rigid dick in one hand like a weapon as with his other hand he pushed my skirt up out of his way.

'God,' he groaned, 'what a beautiful ass...'

I cried out in surprise and pleasure as he spanked me. Both my tender cheeks burned beneath the blow, and the heat surged enticingly down into my pussy. I was deliciously conscious of my soft panties shackling my thighs as I spread my legs just far enough, bracing myself on my thin high-heels as best I could preparing for his peneration. I closed my eyes, and kept them closed; it made me feel even more vulnerably open and exposed, which excited me.

'You want my cock inside you, Ariana?' he asked harshly.

'Yes,' I whispered, afraid he would give me too much time to think. I wanted him to thrust me out of normal space so I was aware only of his pulsing force stroking me and lifting me up on it... I whimpered when I felt the promisingly thick head of his erection kiss the hungry wet heart of my vulva; a kiss that illuminated darker depths inside me than I had ever realized were there. The sensation of his cock plunging into me all at once was unbelievable. He gripped my hips with both hands and began swiftly sliding in and out of me, stretching my tight passage open around his forceful strokes in time with my grateful cries. He fucked me exactly as I had hoped he would and it felt too good for words; I can scarcely describe how fulfilled I felt inside that skeletally furnished room at the back of a locksmith's shop, as though a rock-hard cock was the key to everything when it was driving into me like that. I felt as though he was thrusting himself to a point deep in my flesh where the pleasure was so intense, I knew I wouldn't be able to stand it unless I opened myself up to it absolutely... unless I shed all traces of anxious resistance and relaxed my innermost self around his relentless rhythm, accepting and embracing the power of his erection to ram deeper and deeper into my body... until he was banging me mercilessly, cruelly digging his fingers into my skin for leverage. And just as all my senses came together in the delirious desire to be violently fucked from behind forever, he pulled out of me abruptly, and I moaned beneath the experience of his cum raining down on my ass.

* * *

Finally in route to mami's house, I was talking to myself in disbelief. 'Jesus, I can't believe I did that! My God!' Death was decidedly an Aphrodisiac; I was completely out of control today. Yet maybe it was Miami that was doing it to me, resurrecting my passionate, wildly in-love-with-life nature which seldom had a chance to express itself up North, where people were generally as reserved as life in winter. Did I really have to go back there?

Eric had been as tender with me afterwards as he had been rough during the act. He commanded me not to move while he procured a napkin from the counter, then cleaned his cum off me slowly, clearly enjoying the job of caressing me. Then he gently slid my panties back up my thighs, smoothed down my skirt, and turning me around to face him, he took me in his arms. He didn't kiss me; he simply held me against him for a few moments while I savored the look I had glimpsed in his eyes – an expression of reverence mingled with a ghost of shock, as though he couldn't quite believe what I had let him do, a reaction I found both reassuring and flattering. I, on the other hand, felt utterly fulfilled and relaxed. I would have regretted the experience only if he hadn't been able to fuck me long and hard enough, but he definitely had, and I was happy. Back out in the shop, he carefully wrote his phone number down for me, and I slipped it into my purse with a smile.

'Are you going to call me?' he asked, as vulnerable now as he had been forceful just minutes before.

'Yes,' I promised, not really knowing whether I would or not, I would decide that when I could clearly see my thoughts again through the fog of contentment he had so virally filled me with.

CHAPTER THREE

After a long, hard day (and it had definitely been that!) it always felt wonderful to take my clothes off and toss them aside like so many used up emotions. After the baptism of a long hot shower I would be ready for a fresh start.

I hadn't been able to stop thinking about Gerald Evans; the memory of him had been there at the very heart of my awareness even while another man was banging me from behind. I had only spent a few minutes in Gerald's company, yet already he had branded himself into my feelings the way looking directly at the sun leaves a darkly luminous spot behind my eyelids. The thought of him had been in the back of my mind while they lowered my great aunt into the earth, while I ate and conversed with my relatives in the restaurant, while I flirted with Eric McGregor, and even while the latter fucked me in such a way I had felt all in favor of police brutality.

Before treating myself to that long awaited shower, I forced myself to quickly unpack. Conveniently, mami was over at my grandfather's apartment along with a handful of relatives left over from the funeral, because I barely had enough time to clean up and dress before I had to run out the door again.

I was staying in my old bedroom, which always made me feel a bit claustrophobic since my personality had expanded considerably since I moved out. Yet at the same time there was a soothing quality to its innocent aura, and I emerged from the pink bathtub feeling as beautifully hopeful as Venus rising from her shell. The water pressure was as invigorating as I remembered it, and it was a good twenty minutes before I walked back into the cool bedroom with a white towel wrapped around my wet hair and another towel wrapped around my damp, flushed body. I was very glad I had unpacked, for now my body lotions and facial creams, my perfumes and my make-up, my panties, stockings, clothes and shoes, were all conveniently at my finger tips like the paints and brushes with which I would fashion a masterpiece. I wanted to look good tonight, really good.

I drifted contentedly over to the full-length mirror and tilted it to a flattering angle before opening the towel and spreading it behind me like wings to study my body. Jogging and hiking kept me slender and firm, but my mother's Latin blood was evident in my curves. I actually possessed a waist beneath the generous handfuls of my breasts, and my hips were neither boyish nor maternal, they were, I felt, just right. And my legs... well, men had often commented on my legs, and they had gotten some good exercise today straining to support me beneath a policeman's violent blows...

Smiling, I wrapped the towel around myself again, satisfied with my appearance; it was other aspects of my life that worried me. My beauty and intelligence attracted men, but my intense personality also seemed to scare them away. My last boyfriend had appeared to be an exception to the rule, but that was only because initially we appeared to agree on everything. Once our differences began surfacing – once I began expressing my own opinions and hence challenging his male omniscience – things got rocky fast. After the first little fight, confrontation piled upon confrontation until the end happened like a landslide. With each passing day, I was more and more relieved I had made the decision to leave him, but it wasn't time to think about the past; it was time to begin getting ready for the future.

I thoroughly enjoyed the ritual of preparing myself for a date. When I was in elementary school, I read somewhere that one of the ingredients in expensive eye shadow is powdered fish scales, and ever since then I have perceived nature's sensual beauty in my make-up. Women once had to crush rose petals to make blush. It's a lot easier for us now, but I always like to remind myself of where things come from.

I quickly blow-dried my hair, which turned out full and lustrous without any further effort, then I pinned it up out of the way and, standing naked in front of the bathroom mirror, I began 'putting on my face'. In my opinion, the natural look is best for daytime (I had worn red lipstick today because a funeral is a dramatic affair) but the night calls for a bolder approach. I applied a thin coat of foundation to my face one shade lighter than my skin-tone for a porcelain effect, and followed it up with a silver-white highlighter along my cheekbones I then diffused with a soft, burgundy blush. I barely touched my eyebrows with a dark-brown pencil before beginning on my eyes. Men have often remarked on my eyes as well. In sunlight my irises are a golden-brown, yet at night they appear almost black. I smoothed a light-brown powder over my whole eyelid, enhanced the inner crease with a deep-brown shade, and dusted a gold shimmer shadow beneath my eyebrows. Finally, I lined the inner rim of my eyes with black pencil. Now I was ready for my lips, which were naturally full and required careful application of a burgundy lip pencil I filled in with a matching satin lipstick. The finishing touch was a dab of clear gloss smoothed over my lower lip to enhance its provocative pout.

Back in the bedroom, I moved on to the closet, where I had already hung most of my clothes, and contentedly pondered the problem of what to wear. Fortunately, my garment bag had kept most of my dresses and shirts wrinkle-free. After wearing black-and-white all day, I felt it was time for a splash of color, something to match my lipstick, and I had just the thing – a dark-red sleeveless silk shirt cut classically low, which enhanced both my breasts and my waist when I tucked it into a white skirt that clung loosely to my hips and fell to mid thigh. It was a sexy skirt, but I would also feel comfortable sitting in it. Pantyhose were out of the question, of course, and I selected a pair of white high-heeled sandals that were elegant but comfortable enough to walk in. All that remained to be chosen now was my jewelry, which was easy – a double faux pearl choker, matching drop earrings, and a bracelet for my right wrist. On my left wrist I always wore my gold watch.

Finally, I began filling a matching white purse. I was entering the dating jungle again and equipping my little survival kit for the night. The feeling of mingled excitement and anxiety churning in my womb was all too familiar, but it was particularly intense this evening. Gerald Evans wasn't just some guy I was going out with; I had sensed depths in him that raised the stakes and made me profoundly nervous. I knew nothing about him, yet I was already obsessed with him. 'This isn't good,' I murmured, pulling the pins out of my hair and shaking it loose, but I was smiling.

* * *

Gerald stood framed by the large painting hanging in the window behind him. The artist had flung random waves of color over the canvas which now provided a dramatic contrast to his short-sleeved black button-down shirt and black Dockers. His hands were thrust deep into his pockets as he glanced up and down the street in between looking down at his watch. It was five minutes to eight; she wasn't late yet (he had only just arrived himself five minutes ago) but she wasn't early either. The sun had long since retired behind the pastel buildings and the soft light lingering in the humid air made the street feel like a watercolor come to life. He loved Coral Gables. Tonight, however, his vision was trained like a periscope on the currents of people flowing up and down the sidewalk, and at last he spotted her. Already he recognized that relaxed, confident stride. That's it, he thought, come to daddy. She was wearing red over white – sexuality and innocence all wrapped up into one irresistible package. He turned his eyes up towards the heavens for a grateful instant, and then began walking towards her.

* * *

In Coral Gables, all the streets have names not numbers, but I knew Andalucia was only a couple of blocks away now. I had walked all the way from mami's house, about three-quarters of a mile. The temperature was ideal, especially when cool gusts of wind coming from the direction of the ocean played with my hair and slipped up my skirt to caress my thighs. I thought of Boston's frigid wind tunnels and paralyzing wind-chill factors (often on the wrong side of zero degrees) and shuddered inwardly. The sky above the old world Spanish-style buildings had gone from the loveliest blue imaginable to a luminous violet that just happened to be my favorite color...

'Ariana.'

The deep, quiet voice brought my eyes down from the sky, to a man's tall body in a black shirt and pants like an exciting evocation of the night waiting beyond the delicate violet veil. 'Gerald,' I gasped because I had almost walked right past him in my celestial contemplation.

His smile deepened. 'I'd love to know what you were thinking just now, Ariana.'

'Oh, I was just admiring the color of the sky. You never see shades of violet so subtle anywhere else.' We began walking in the direction of the gallery.

'I guess you've never been to the desert,' he remarked. 'In the desert the entire horizon can be a whole shimmering spectrum of violet, purple and lavender colors impossible to describe... colors so beautiful you almost feel as though you're looking at a magical portal into another world.'

From the moment I met him my instincts had told me this man meant every word he said, so his poetic description wasn't just calculated to impress me. 'What desert was that?' I asked earnestly.

'The Sahara, in Egypt.'

I sighed. 'I've always wanted to go to Egypt! But is it safe these days?'

'As safe as anything else in life.' He held the gallery door open for me, and I preceded him into the cold, shadowy interior where all the lights hung inwardly over individual paintings. The small space was crowded, but the atmosphere was formally hushed. He took my arm, and guided me towards a young man in a white waiter's jacket who was walking around with a tray of little plastic champagne glasses. His fingers were warm against my bare skin, and his grip was somehow both polite and possessive. My awareness of his hand was the only thing that mattered; everything else in the room felt like a dream in which only his touch was real.

I accepted the glass of champagne he handed me. 'Thank you.' I smiled up at him.

He touched his plastic rim to mine. He seemed about to say something, because one of his dimples deepened like a period at the end of a silent sentence, but he merely sipped the sparkling wine.

'What?' I asked. The champagne was a bit flat and tepid, but I didn't mind.

'What?' he echoed.

'You were about to say something…'

'I was?'

'Yes, you were.'

His smile deepened. 'I think you heard me.'

I couldn't seem to feel the floor beneath my feet when he looked at me that way.

He touched his glass to mine again, then drained it. 'Maybe this wasn't such a good idea,' he said abruptly.

My heart seemed to stop. 'What do you mean?'

His eyes fell to my painted toe nails in white-strapped sandals, traveled slowly up my legs, then my breasts, and finally came to rest on my face again. 'It's hard to look at anything else with you around, Ariana.'

I felt exactly the same way about him. 'We should make an effort.'

'Whatever you like.'

It was an effort to turn away from him, but I managed to move over to a wall dominated by a large, realistically surreal work. The naked man in the dark foreground was facing into the painting, half lying down, half sitting, as if he had just woken up. He was staring up at a canvas resting on an easel before him, the painting inside the painting depicting a flesh-colored maze.

'This one's rather interesting,' I commented. It didn't hurt that the man was beautiful, slender and muscular. I glanced at Gerald, suddenly a little embarrassed. The way he wore his clothes told me it could easily be him in the painting.

'You really like it?' he asked seriously.

'Yes, I do.' I drained my glass.

He immediately took it from me and I watched him walk over to a waste basket. He moved like a man who was comfortable with the fact that he was attractive, but he did not seem obsessed by his looks. There was nothing self-consciously pretentious about him; his spine was sensually relaxed, not stiffly conceited.

Returning to my side, he rested his right hand lightly on the small of my back, and we walked over to another painting that looked like a photograph of a river and trees seen from some unlikely bird's eye perspective.

He bent over and whispered in my ear, 'Do you like this one, Ariana?'

'No,' I replied at once, but I definitely liked the feel of his breath against my skin. I had tucked my hair behind my ear to keep it out of my eye, and suddenly imagining his warm tongue tracing its seashell-like curves made me feel weak in the knees.

'Why don't you like it?' he insisted.

'Because it's not saying anything.'

'To you.'

'To anyone.' I became passionate. 'It's not expressing a vision of the world, it's just copying it. I mean, obviously the artist is an excellent craftsman, but,' I shrugged, 'where's the mystery? It doesn't intrigue me. It doesn't draw me in… I don't know, I just don't like it.'

'I don't like it either. Let's get out of here.'

My left hand brushed his right one as we turned towards the door, and the contact set off a devastating series of explosions in my nerve-endings. Before I knew it, my slender fingers had slipped between his strong ones and I had absolutely no desire to untangle them even as my mind warned me it was much too soon to be feeling this way. Then he gave my hand a gentle squeeze, and I suffered the impression he was reassuring me; telling me it was all right, that he didn't think less of me for so quickly succumbing to the inevitable. In fact, I was sure he respected me for not playing games and pretending I didn't want him to touch me.

We stepped outside into a current of gallery-going pedestrians. I quickly scanned the crowd for any potential competition, and was pleased not to spot any. There were quite a few young women on the street dressed to the hilt, and more mature, elegant ladies in tight black pants and dresses, but with my hand in Gerald's, I was the night's undisputed queen.

'Are those sandals comfortable to walk in, Ariana?'

'Yes, that's why I bought them.'

'Not because your legs look great in them?'

We smiled at each other again.

My God, I thought, this can't be happening! I tried to figure out exactly what was happening, but I couldn't think past the happiness consuming me. My veins felt like fuses this man had lit all at once without warning.

We went to three more galleries on the same block and agreed there really wasn't much of interest in any of them. Wonderfully enough, we seemed to share a similar taste in art. The only piece we both lingered over was a life-sized sculpture.

Two prostrate figures struggled to emerge from a single piece of black stone where they were caught in the act of making love. The man's arms were straight and ribbed with muscles, forming two columns on either side of the woman, whose face was raised to his in a passionate kiss, and yet the place where their bodies merged was a smooth, peaceful darkness.

'Wow,' I whispered reverently, 'this is beautiful!'

'You think it's beautiful?'

I glanced at him. Three faint lines were traced into his forehead as he stared at the piece.

'Of all the things we've seen tonight, this is the only one that's really grabbed me,' I declared fervently.

His eyes met mine briefly, almost shyly. 'Really?' He looked back at the stone couple as though he couldn't quite figure out how he felt about them.

'Yes, really, but then again, I'm slightly biased towards sculptures,' I confessed.

He gave me his full attention. 'And why is that?'

'Because I like to work with clay in my spare time.'

'You like to work with clay in your spare time,' he repeated slowly, as though I had spoken another language he was translating to himself. Then he frowned. 'You sculpt?'

'Um, not really, I just like playing with clay. I love art, but I'm primarily a word person.'

'So you're a writer?' His tone was almost interrogative.

'Yes.' Not in the mood to talk about my job, and anxious to drop a subject that for some reason seemed to disturb him, I walked away towards a painting.

He fell into stride beside me. 'You're an artist?' His quiet voice sounded incredulous.

'What's so hard to believe about that?' I snapped, my Cuban temper surging up for an instant. 'I mean, just because I'm–'

'There's nothing hard to believe about it at all, Ariana.' The way he smiled down into my eyes made me completely forget what I had been about to say. 'I should have known you weren't just beautiful on the surface,' he added in an undertone as though talking to himself.

'Why?' I was compelled to inquire just as quietly.

He reached up and lightly traced one of my cheekbones with two slightly rough fingertips. It was intoxicating the way his eyes looked straight down into mine as he smiled. His dark-gray irises were infinitely soft, yet the personality behind them was strong, and my body responded to it with an irresistible warmth spreading up from between my thighs into my womb. He asked, 'Are you hungry?'

I nodded, not trusting myself to speak.

CHAPTER FOUR

When I got home later, mami was waiting for me on the couch as though I was still fifteen-years-old and had been out on my first date. She was wearing a new multi-colored silk robe that in my euphoric state made me think of a stained glass window melted around her by the warmth of her spirit. I thought of saints rescued from a cold church resting against her soft skin as I sat down beside her.

'Well?' she demanded, frowning slightly as she took in my flushed cheeks and beatific smile.

'Well what?' I sing-songed.

'You flew down for a funeral and you're already in love?' she accused.

'Love and death walk hand-in-hand,' I declared inanely.

She crossed her arms as if to defend herself from trite sayings, and settled determinedly back against the cushion. 'Is he another American?'

I sighed and tossed the hair out of my eye. The question had the effect of a needle bursting my euphoric bubble, and yet, to my surprise, I found that my heart still felt wonderfully full. Search as I might, I couldn't seem to find a single doubt about Gerald in my mind.

It was Rosa's turn to sigh, with exaggerated patience, as she waited for me to snap out of my reverie and face the usual firing squad of questions. In her mind, this man, and my possible relationship with him, was condemned to death until time proved otherwise, as it never yet had, unfortunately.

'Mami,' I said firmly, 'I don't want to talk about him yet.'

'Why not?'

'I just can't…'

'Why, is there something about him you don't want me to know? He's…' She uncrossed her arms as she sat up. 'He's not married is he?!'

I winced; panic had raised her voice several decibels right next to my ear. 'Of course not, you know I would never get involved with a married man. That's like buying a one-way ticket to the moon.'

She laughed, more with relief than at my silly image.

'He's different, mami,' I said fervently, looking straight into her eyes willing her to believe what I saw in this man – the very real possibility that everything I had ever dreamed of could come true with him. Then I added the clincher, 'His father's side of the family is from Northern Italy.'

'Well, why didn't you say so?' She slapped my thigh by way of an affectionate reprimand. I also knew it reminded her of the time when I was a baby and we could be innocently warm and close to each other physically. 'When can I meet him?'

'Soon,' I replied truthfully. 'I want to have him over for dinner.'

'Where did you go tonight?'

'Just Houston's. I was in the mood for one of their burgers.'

'With so many little excellent Italian restaurants to choose from you went to Houstons?!'

Mami is the Italy buff to end all Italy buffs, and she had literally been there ten times whereas I had yet to set foot on this other perfect planet where the need for beauty in all things was as real as the law of gravity everywhere else. 'I wanted a burger, okay?'

'Hmm, listening to you talk no one would know you're a gourmet cook.'

Recognizing one of the conversational dead ends I often ran into with my mother, I stood up. 'I'm going to bed,' I announced as the euphoric force-field left over from my evening with Gerald suddenly gave way beneath a flash of exhaustion. 'It's been a long day.'

'Ay, si, pobresita, hasta mañana.' She got up to hug me. 'I'm so glad you're here, Ari.' She didn't ask me how long I could stay, but somehow I felt the question expressed in the wordless sentences of her arms, along with the weak but stubborn hope that maybe Gerald would make her dream come true by getting me to move back down to Miami.

* * *

In a dark bedroom in Coral Gables, Gerald is sitting naked at his desk in a big red leather chair he found next to the 'magic dumpster', as he calls it, because whatever he needs invariably materializes beside it. He sent a wish out to the universe for a comfortable and elegant leather chair to match his hand-made wooden desk, and the very next day there it was, lording it over a pile of trash bags like a dispossessed nobleman surrounded by a group of humbly bowing serfs. The supple leather now cushioned his bare backside, and a penis impressively large even at rest as he surfed the Net. Efficiently using two fingers on his black keyboard, he swiftly typed the name "Ariana Padron" and unconsciously held his breath… a list of websites immediately scrolled down the nineteen-inch screen, bathing his handsome features and bare chest in a white electronic light. Tonight, there was no one there to see his firm mouth soften into a smile as he selected one of her short stories at random, knowing it would reveal more to him than the articles she had been paid to write, and began reading…

Gerald devoured three of Arian's stories because reading her words felt like caressing her innermost self and getting to know her better. Her absence was already almost a physical pain for him, and this way he was at least learning what she liked and didn't like, what her hopes and fears were, what she desired… he came to understand that she had a profound, almost unshakable, faith in the divine mystery of her existence coupled with a healthy respect for her sensuality; she embraced the gift of her senses like profound clues to the ultimate secrets of her nature. Yet, blessedly, her light-hearted attitude was the antithesis of fanaticism – a pure nakedness of being that refused to wear any one particular belief or dogma. He knew Ariana had found what she was looking for. All she needed was a man to give full glorious form to her desires and to smooth out her doubts and fears. All Ariana Padron needed, Gerald decided firmly, was him.

* * *

The first thing I always did when I came home to visit was make sure there was food in the house. Mami's refrigerator was always painfully empty except for staples like Cuban coffee, bread and sugar. Fortunately, that was enough to fortify me for a trip to the local supermarket. I went alone; grocery shopping with Rosa was like dragging a ball-and-chain down the isles rattling complaints, 'Are we finished yet?' 'Do we really need so much stuff?' 'Can't we just eat out tonight?' etc. etc. I had long since given up trying to inspire in my mother the sense of awe I experience whenever I walk into a good grocery store. How can I not be thankful I'm one of those people fortunate enough to have the fruits of the earth laid effortlessly at my fingertips? Yes, I work for the money with which I buy them, and I don't make all that much money really, yet inconceivable numbers of human beings work and slave for next to nothing at all, starving and dying despite all their best efforts to survive. In my eyes, a big clean neatly stocked supermarket feels almost like a Cathedral reminding me how blessed I am to be where I am and who I am. It makes me imagine I'm a sorceress possessed of endless ingredients to work magic with, and the purer the ingredient, the more effective my culinary spells will be.

I bought the essentials needed to survive at my mother's house and more… after all, there was Gerald's appetite to consider now… and the tantalizingly forceful taste left on my sexual palate by the Viking with the handcuffs was also still tentatively on my list as worth exploring; his phone number was beginning to burn a hole in my purse. I knew either one of these men would take me out to dinner again if that's what I wanted, but perversely enough I fantasized about feeding them myself, especially Gerald, even though it still seriously worried me how relaxed and happy I had felt with him last night. As I pushed my cart down the aisle, I kept telling myself it was too soon, too soon… even as I splurged on three Filet Mignons. I thanked all the lords above he wasn't a Vegan like my brother, whom I love dearly, but we will never see eye-to-eye when it comes to food since one of my ideas of hell (I have several) is having to give up cheese forever.

I spent more than I should have, but then as usual I reminded myself that eating out was infinitely more expensive than indulging my gourmet hobby, and I was content again as I drove back to mami's house. The unforgiving heat and sunlight outside were still a shock to my system; it was a relief to get out of the car's hot oven (it didn't have enough time to cool off during the short drive back from the supermarket) and begin carrying heavy bags into the refrigerated house.

'Por Dios, Ariana!' my mother exclaimed after my third trip back out to the car.

I kicked the front door closed behind me. 'I don't need your help, thank you,' I said, which translated into, 'Stay out of the kitchen and out of my way.'

Still in her stained-glass robe, Rosa shrugged philosophically. 'Whatever you say.' She eyed the explosion of life-filled plastic bags at her feet with distaste. 'Did you remember to buy crackers?' she asked suspiciously.

'Yes, and now I'm going to put all this away.' I marched towards the kitchen carrying as many bags as I could lift. 'Then I'm going to make you some healthy things to snack on. You can't live on just crackers, hot chocolate and canned tuna.' What I planned to prepare are three things I always have available at home: Low Fat Hummus, Tofu Spinach Artichoke Dip and Tofu Cheddar Cheese Sauce.

It's wonderful when my love of indulgent "comfort" food happily marries my desire to eat right in nutritional paradise. My version of the Middle Eastern dip uses less Sesame Tahini and Olive Oil than traditionally called for, drastically reducing the fat content.

LOWER-FAT ROASTED GARLIC HUMMUS

1 16 oz can Garbanzo Beans, drained and very well rinsed (this helps reduce the high sodium content of canned beans and vegetables)
1 tsp Sea Salt
2 tsp minced Roasted Garlic*
2 Tbls Sesame Tahini (can be found in health food stores and some major grocery stores, but be sure not to confuse it with prepared Tahini Dip)

3 Tbls bottled Lemon Juice or 1/4 cup Fresh Lemon Juice
(recommended)
2-3 Tbls Water
Extra Virgin Olive Oil
1-2 Chopped Green Onions (Optional)
1/4 cup chopped Black Olives (Optional)

Combine all the ingredients except the Green Onions and
Black Olives in a medium-sized plastic container, stir well
with a spoon, then puree the mixture with a hand-held
blender – a great tool designed for pureeing soups while
still in the pan that's much easier to clean than a food
processor. Add the chopped Green Onions and/or the
Black Olives. If the mixture seems too thick, pour in
another tablespoon or two of water. A thinner consistency
works best for dips, but for sandwiches you'll want the
mixture to be a bit thicker. Cover the container and refrigerate it for up to one week.

*If you can't find Roasted Garlic minced and bottled at
your supermarket, it's easy to make your own. Just brush a
whole head of garlic with some olive oil and bake it in a
400° oven for about 45 minutes. You want it brown but not
black, and it's a synch to peel the dried skin off the cloves
once they've cooled a bit. They also freeze beautifully, so
you can always have some roasted garlic on hand when you
want it. You can make Hummus with regular minced garlic, but the results are not quite as mouth-watering.

As an appetizer, dip raw carrots and celery sticks into your
Hummus or enjoy it with Organic Corn Chips – stone-ground

corn, sea salt and oil (absolutely not hydrogenated oil). Hummus makes great sandwiches and roll-ups, too. You can use any combination of ingredients you prefer, but this one really works for me:

WONDROUS WRAP

1 large Whole Wheat Wrap Bread
Home-Made Hummus
Some Baby Carrots, finely chopped
1 chopped Plum Tomato
A generous sprinkling of crumbled Feta Cheese
Broccoli Sprouts and/or Salad Greens sprinkled with pepper

Spread everything evenly across the Wrap Bread leaving a one inch border, then slowly begin rolling the bread closed from one side like a carpet, pushing the filling in with your fingertips as you go. It's tricky and messy and not for the faint of heart, but it can be done! Fold in the ends, then triumphantly slice on the diagonal with a very sharp knife. If you're taking it to work for lunch, wrap it tightly in tin foil; the ingredients will consolidate very nicely.

TOFU SPINACH ARTICHOKE DIP

1/2 package (about 9 oz) Soft Tofu, pureed
1 8-9 oz container Light (preferably whipped) Cream Cheese, at room temperature
1 1/2- 2 cups frozen chopped Spinach, thawed and drained with paper towels
1 16 oz can Artichoke Hearts, chopped
1 cup Soy Parmesan Cheese
1 1/2 tsp Garlic Powder

1/4 tsp Red Hot Pepper Flakes
1 tsp Salt
Freshly ground Black Pepper

Combine all the ingredients in a large bowl, then stir well and thoroughly to mix. This really couldn't be easier to make and you simply won't believe how good it tastes or that it's actually good for you. Heat the dip until it's good and hot (I use a microwave) and enjoy it with Organic Corn Chips or whatever else you prefer.

TOFU CHEDDAR CHEESE SAUCE

1 Package (about 18 oz) Soft Tofu
1/2 cup Organic (high quality, low sodium) Chicken Broth
2/3 cup grated Extra Sharp Cheddar Cheese
1/4 cup grated American Cheese
1 Tbls Butter, thinly sliced
1 tsp Dijon Mustard
1 1/2 tsp Sea Salt
Fresh ground Pepper

If you don't have a hand-held blender (I highly recommend the small investment; they're only about ten dollars) use a food processor or a blender to puree the Tofu, then add the Chicken Broth and blend until smooth. You want a creamy sauce that's not too thick but not too thin either. In a microwave- safe bowl, heat the mixture uncovered for 3-4 minutes, and then quickly add the grated Cheeses plus the tablespoon of Butter, stirring to melt and blend with a wooden spoon. Finally, add the Mustard, Salt and Pepper. You can refrigerate the sauce for several hours. When you're ready to serve, heat it in a microwave for 2-3 minutes and pour it over hot macaroni, bow-tie or ziti pasta. This recipe makes enough for one pound of pasta.* This is also a great healthy topping for steamed cauliflower or broccoli that freezes very nicely in small portions.

*Low-Carb pasta is right up there with fat-free cheese on the culinary most wanted list for criminal offense against the taste buds. If you're watching your carbohydrate intake, but also care about truly enjoying everything you put in your mouth and swallow, simply refrain from eating pasta altogether. Or try whole wheat pasta, which gives your body the fiber it needs and craves through such wonderful substances as whole grain breads and legumes. The fact is that keeping your body feeling fit and therefore feeling sexy goes hand-in-hand with maintaining a healthy weight no matter what all the quick-fix diet cults say. An extreme diet may work for quick, short-term weight loss, but in the end pleasurably balanced eating coupled with regular exercise is the only path that offers a life-long sense of well-being.

CHAPTER FIVE

After fixing some healthy snacks for mami, I made sure to leave the kitchen nice and tidy behind me for the next time I would use it, because it dampens my creative energy being forced to clean up the dregs of my previous culinary spell before dreaming up another one. There were certain routines I had developed living alone that I stuck to religiously in the belief that sensually enjoyable rituals are a stabilizing force. Some of my friends called it 'getting into a rut' but it's all a matter of perspective. Speaking of which, I realized I had completely lost my objective perspective on Gerald. The whole time I was in the kitchen, I kept waiting for the phone to ring even while pretending not to, and now that I'd finished my self-imposed tasks, the fact that he still had not called was nagging at me like a predatory bird picking at Prometheus' heart; I had been foolish to get all fired up about a complete stranger. Granted, it was still early in the day and he was probably busy, which thought caused another worry to darken my swiftly fading happiness – I had spent hours with the man last night and yet I still had no idea what he did for a living. I hadn't even noticed how suavely he had gotten me to talk about myself most of the time. It wasn't that I hadn't been curious about him, and thinking about it now, it dawned on me that I hadn't asked him a lot of specific questions about his work because I felt it didn't matter at all what he did for a living; whatever his career, he was an intensely interesting person I had thoroughly enjoyed spending time with.

Mami had gone to meet a friend for lunch on Miracle Mile. Naturally, she had wanted me to go with her, but I begged off. I prefer only to have a light snack for lunch, and I was in no mood to be grilled about my love life. So here I was alone in my childhood home, which felt painfully like a snail's shell I had outgrown as time suddenly began dragging more slowly than seemed possible. I had personally proved the relativity of time on countless occasions while waiting for a man to whom I was irresistibly drawn to call me…

I didn't consciously intend to search the black depths of my purse for the white fragment of paper on which Eric had written his phone number, but I did, and there it was. Having some calling power myself made me feel better for a few seconds, but then thinking about another man only made me ache to see Gerald again even more. Well, he had both mami's number and my cell phone number; I had given him everything I could for now.

* * *

I spent the rest of the day recovering from the previous day even while engaged in the mysteriously strenuous exercise of trying to relax and pretend not to care if Gerald ever called me or not. It would have been easier to run a five hour marathon. Pride be damned, I cared very much whether Gerald called me again or not, and by six o'clock – after I checked my work e-mail several times, read three chapters of the novel I was currently devouring, fixed myself a hummus sandwich on whole wheat bread, and enjoyed a brief but deliciously deep cat-nap – I was so upset I hadn't heard from him that I picked up the phone on my night-stand, snatched up the paper with Eric's phone number on it as I sat up in bed, and dialed it. Part of me felt strangely weightless, as though I was adrift in an empty universe and had deliberately entered coordinates in my navigational system that would take me to the completely wrong planet only because the world I was striving to reach was, for some terrible reason, not responding.

'Yeah?'

My breath caught. I hadn't really expected him to answer. 'Eric?' I asked stupidly.

'Ariana…'

The almost vulnerable way he said my name made me feel bet-ter for an instant I desperately took advantage of before I could regret calling him. 'Still feel like that drink, Eric?'

'Sure. I'm on my way home, but it won't take me long to show-er and change. How about if I pick you up at eight? If you give me your–'

'Let's just meet somewhere. I feel like taking a walk… how about if we rendezvous at the Colannade Hotel bar at eight o'clock?'

'I'll be there.'

'Great.' I hoped my voice didn't sound too flat. I switched off the phone, and collapsed back across my pillows. Now, of course, Gerald would call because I had made other plans, plans I would not hesitate to break, but that wasn't the point; the point was now that I was technically not just waiting around for him to get in touch with me, he would. I should have known better than to think

I could trick the universe. While I showered and changed, while I put on my make-up and brushed my hair, both telephones remained stubbornly silent. Making sure it was fully charged, I put my cell-phone in my purse, where for a few seconds it glowed with a violet light expressive of my deepest hope. Then, grateful mami still hadn't returned and I didn't have to answer any questions, I walked out the door to go meet one man because I couldn't handle how much I longed to see another.

* * *

It was still uncomfortably warm outside, but the cruel sun had descended to play with a final mellow burst of energy in the jungle-like backyards of my mother's street. Most of the homes were hidden behind private stone walls over which only the branches of old trees were visible. When my parents split up long ago, my dad left mami the house, which had since become infinitely more valuable, and its worth just kept going up astronomically. Coral Gable's residential backstreets are a peaceful green oasis in Miami's stressful concrete desert, and being able to live here was only a financial mirage for me; I couldn't actually afford it, and moving back home was totally out of the question. As I walked – enjoying the evening breeze caressing the hot, damp nape of my neck when I lifted my hair up with both hands – I was resigned to the fact that I would have to move back up to my rent-control apartment in Boston. I had forgotten it's a good idea to put your hair up when you decide to walk anywhere in Miami, but it was too late now and, anyway, I didn't give a damn if my hair was a mess when I got to the bar or not. With every step I took my mood became more and more glum. I had sincerely believed Gerald enjoyed my company last night as much as I enjoyed his, but his twenty-four hour silence felt like a killing frost to my instincts. I was forced to consider the possibility I had only imagined our intense attraction to each other. Maybe part of me was more upset by my recent break-up than I realized. Obviously, I had been unconsciously searching for a net to break my fall, and I had chosen an enigmatic stranger from a funeral home. I didn't even want to think about my slutty behavior in the locksmith's shop, yet there was no denying to myself it was one of the reasons I was walking to the Colannade Hotel now. If I dated Eric for as long as I was in Miami, I would feel a little less guilty about what I had let him do to me when he was still essentially a total stranger.

I emerged from the quiet backstreet onto the 42nd Avenue sidewalk wondering just how many little games I played with myself mentally and emotionally I wasn't consciously aware of. The roaring, surging traffic made me stop at the intersection as I waited for the light to change, yet at the same time I was going entirely against my inner signals. My intuition kept flashing red for Eric – I wasn't truly interested in him, he was a dead end and I knew it – and glowing green for Gerald – he could be the one to help me go where I had always dreamed of going in a relationship. Obviously, I was color blind!

I made it across the street in one piece after more than one car blasted its horn – a primitive mating call many Miami males still indulge in, not having yet evolved enough to realize it's a complete turn-off. Every step I took made me almost uncomfortably aware of my heart beating faster and harder the longer I walked and the longer the phone in my purse remained distressingly dead. I tried to entertain myself by imagining how I would react if Gerald finally called me just as I was sitting down for a drink with Eric, but I couldn't picture that happening, which upset me even more. I've learned from experience that if

I can't imagine something happening, it doesn't; either that or it happens in a completely different way than I could ever have expected judging from the available evidence. Somehow I knew beyond a shadow of a doubt that Gerald would not call me while I was with Eric, so the closer I got to my destination, the more hopeless I felt. Nevertheless, it was a relief to finally step into the Collande air conditioned lobby, where a black-and-white marble floor and a working stone fountain in the center all contributed to making me feel wonderfully cool and refreshed physically despite the heat of my inner turmoil.

I knew from shopping on Miracle Mile that the Colannade boasts a lovely bathroom beneath the main staircase leading up to the reception desk, and I swiftly clicked my way towards it in my black strap sandals, which I had chosen because they had small, comfortable heals for walking. I hadn't been inspired to dress for this assignation, in fact, my mood was fashionably black. As I stepped into the spacious marble bathroom, I found it vaguely amusing that I was dressed more appropriately for a funeral this evening than I had been yesterday. I had taken great care over my appearance for Gerald, but for Eric I had almost indifferently slipped into a sleeveless cotton dress that clung ever so gently to my curves as it fell to just above my knees. I rarely ever wear a bra, and especially in Miami's sticky heat it felt nice to let my breasts bob up and down, my nipples poking against the fabric caressing them making me feel vibrantly lovely and alive.

I had just opened my purse to pull out my hairbrush when my cell-phone rang at last. I gasped in surprise. I'm ashamed to say I had pretty much given up hope, and my heart started racing as an enchanted lavender light flooded the leather's black depths. The contents of my purse had shifted while I walked, and it took me three agonizing rings to fish out my phone.

'Hello?' I said calmly.

'The word hello didn't exist before the telephone, you know.'

'Yes, as a matter-of-fact, I did know that.' My reflection smiled at me as if saying I knew he'd call, but you're stupid and always worry too much!

'Of course you knew. You're the smartest, most beautiful woman I've ever met.'

'Oh, come now…'

'Not now, but soon, I hope.'

Suddenly in need of support, I turned and leaned against the counter. 'I was beginning to think you weren't going to call,' I confessed reluctantly.

'Now why on earth would you think that?'

'Because I really wanted you to call, Gerald…' I hadn't planned on revealing my insecurity to him, but as had happened last night at dinner, I couldn't seem to hold anything back from this man; I had no desire to keep anything from him because I was sure he would understand whatever I said and, I suspected, help me understand it better myself.

'You should have known I would call you, Ariana.' His tone was at once stern and tender, a combination I loved so much I closed my eyes for a second in disbelief that such a man was real and talking to me on the phone. 'Unfortunately,' he went on, 'I already had plans for tonight I can't get out of, but I'd like to see you again tomorrow night, if that's all right with you.'

I glanced at my watch willing the hands to fast-forward twenty-four hours in obedience of my heart pulsing as if at the speed of light I was so happy and relieved and excited and terrified all at the same time. 'Of course it's all right,' I heard myself say. 'Would you like to come over for dinner?'

'You don't have to cook for me, Ariana, I'd be happy to–'

'I know I don't have to, Gerald, it would be my pleasure to fix us dinner.'

'Then it would be my pleasure to accept your invitation. I assume your mother will be there since you're staying with her?'

'Um, yes...'

'Wonderful, I can thank her for making sure you were born on earth at the same time I was.'

I laughed even though it worried me how happy his little joke made me. 'Maybe next time I can cook dinner for you at your place,' I dared to suggest.

'Well...'

I held my breath against an encroaching wave of despair... he was married or he lived with someone...

'I'd love that, but I'll have to... clean up a bit first.'

I sighed and mentally chided myself for once again jumping to a negative conclusion.

'You see, I use my kitchen for storage,' he admitted.

'Storage?'

'Yes, the oven's a great place to put books.'

'You keep books in your oven?'

'Yes, they're really hot reading.'

I giggled. My elation was the emotional equivalent of a champagne glass dangerously close to overflowing. Yet this inexpressibly rare vintage of feeling I had finally met the right man was to be wasted on someone else, for I was already late for my date with Eric.

'I'll call you for directions tomorrow,' he said.

'Okay.'

'Good night, beautiful.'

'Good night...'

'I really wish I could get out of this thing tonight,' he added abruptly, 'but I can't.'

'It's all right, I understand.'

'No, you don't, but you will. It's because I want to see you so much that I have to go somewhere else tonight.'

This was a vital riddle I suspected I would spend most of the evening digesting, but at the moment it tasted infinitely sweet because my heart seemed to know just what it meant. 'I'm glad, Gerald.'

'So am I, Ariana. I'll talk to you tomorrow. Good night.'

'Good night.'

I waited until I heard him hang up before I turned back towards the rose-and-black marble counter, and reverently placed the cool body of my phone back in my purse.

* * *

I considered standing Eric up, but I couldn't do it. It was too late; I was already there. Besides, I told myself, what was the harm in simply having a drink with him when we had already done something much more intimate? I was blissfully happy knowing I was going to see Gerald again, so I was smiling as I walked into the hotel bar. I immediately spotted Eric's magnificent physique rising from one of the small golden couches to greet me, and there was nothing I could do about it if he thought my expression was all for him. He was wearing the same pair of dangerously tight jeans into which he had tucked a short-sleeved white t-shirt that clung to his pecs in a stunningly sexy way; nevertheless, it turned me off with the possibility he spent more time lifting weights than exercising his intellect.

'Hello, beautiful,' he greeted me soberly.

I wondered why it had felt so different when Gerald called me 'beautiful' just minutes before. 'Hi,' I replied lightly, selfishly resting my hands on his muscular arms for an instant to give him a sisterly kiss on the cheek. I didn't like the intensely serious way he was looking at me; it made me feel guilty about having called him in my impatient obsession with another man's call.

'Is this all right?' He indicated the couch behind him. 'Or would you rather sit at the bar?'

'No, this is perfect,' I declared, seating myself, 'although I liked it better when they had black leather chairs and sofas in here.' I set my purse on the cushion between us as I crossed my legs and turned towards him slightly even while keeping my distance. 'The décor is just a bit too... yellow now.'

He followed the smooth length of my legs from where the hem of my dress rested against my thigh all the way down to the web-like straps of my sandals, where his vision was caught for a long moment. 'You have unbelievable legs, Ariana.'

'Thank you,' I replied airily, very glad Gerald had refrained from verbally admiring my legs, which made him stand out from other men even more. I certainly don't mind compliments, but I also don't relish feeling like a collection of body parts all being judged separately.

Eric met my eyes, and said more than I wanted to hear by remaining silent.

I looked away, ostensibly searching the lounge for a waiter.

'He'll be back in a minute,' my date informed me quietly. 'How long will you be in Miami?'

For a second I debated lying to him, but I'm a terrible liar. 'I'm not sure,' I said truthfully, then regretted it. It seemed obvious my uncertainty involved a man, and naturally he would think it was him. 'But I bought a roundtrip ticket, so I probably won't be here long,' I added awkwardly, resting one of my hands on my purse and the other on the arm of the couch. I told myself I was only imagining the glint of anger in his unusually clear eyes... eyes that disturbingly evoked a predatory animal's stare never darkened by the conscience of a soul…

'So where do you live?' he asked almost harshly. 'Do you have a boyfriend?'

'You sound like you're interrogating me.' I laughed. 'Have I committed a crime, officer?'

'Yes, you have, Ariana.' He seemed about to reach for my hand, but instead he abruptly lifted his cute denim-clad ass off the couch, and thrust his hand into one of his front pockets. 'Here…' He extracted a small black-velvet box from his pants and casually tossed it into my lap. 'I noticed yesterday that your ears were pierced.'

'Eric, you shouldn't have…' The case contained two small gold hoop earrings. 'They're lovely, thank you.' I refrained from mentioning I preferred silver. 'But you shouldn't have.' I looked regretfully into his eyes.

'Why not?' he demanded quietly.

I was saved from having to answer by the arrival of the waiter. I ordered a glass of Chardonnay, and Eric confirmed my conviction that there was no possible future between us by ordering a coke, even though I had to admire him for obeying one of the laws he helped enforce by not drinking and driving himself. 'So, what crime have I committed?' I asked curiously, closing the jewel box afraid he would ask me to put the earrings on, which to a superstitious part of my brain would have constituted a betrayal of my swiftly deepening feelings for Gerald. The golden hoops would symbolically keep me in Eric's orbit; my superficial evanescent attraction to him would mock the precious, timeless metal and wreak havoc with the mysterious laws of energy surrounding me, bringing me bad luck with the man I truly desired…

'You've committed the crime of making me want you,' he stated bluntly. 'More than I've ever wanted a woman.'

'But you've already had me,' I teased cruelly.

He picked up my purse and set it on the table in front of us. 'Come here,' he said in such a way that my body slid across the couch towards him of its own volition, before my mind even had the chance to protest. 'Put them on for me,' he commanded, slipping an arm around my shoulders, and his physical proximity suddenly made me feel limp as a puppet whose movements he was now controlling as I was forced to set aside my symbolic fears and obey him. I opened the jewel case again, caught one of the fragile golden hoops between my fingertips, and tossed my hair back as I brought it up to my ear. Years of experience enabled me to easily find the tiny hole in my earlobe. 'Very nice,' he whispered after I had slipped them both on.

'Thank you,' I said tensely, because my body was inevitably, traitorously, responding to the visceral memory of how hard he had fucked me.

Our drinks arrived just as my cell-phone came alive again, the urgent ring muffled by my purse and its contents. 'Excuse me, I have to get that,' I said, disengaging myself from him. This time, five nerve-shattering rings went by before I was able to answer. I had dreaded it might be Gerald again, so when I saw Mami on the display, I was infinitely relieved.

'Hi,' I said cheerfully.

'Where are you?' she demanded.

'At the Colannade Hotel.'

'And what are you doing there? Are you with that man again... what was his name? Are you planning to spend any time with your mother while you're here?'

'Yes, I'm going to spend time with you, mami, but I can't talk right now. I'll be home soon, I promise.' I quickly switched off the phone. 'That was my mom,' I informed Eric.

'I gathered as much.'

I dropped the phone back in my purse, deliberately setting it between us again, and reached for my Chardonnay feeling I had earned it (I feel that way every day after six o'clock). I sipped the golden liquid gratefully, avoiding Eric's eyes as I conjured up a lie. 'I'm afraid I'm condemned to have dinner with a bunch of my relatives tonight.' I almost believed it myself.

'Well.' He downed half his coke in one thirsty (angry?) swallow. 'Do you have time to join me for a little appetizer, at least?'

'Certainly.'

'Good, I know of a little place around the corner. Finish your wine.'

'Yes, sir,' I teased soberly. At that moment, everything about him looked so hard I couldn't resist a primal desire to obey him; a basic instinct aroused in me by the heady aura of authority surrounding him I knew from experience he wouldn't hesitate to enforce. I wondered what restaurant he had in mind, but for some reason I didn't ask. I simply entertained myself watching him pull his wallet out of a back pocket, admiring his ass again as he tossed some cash onto the table next to his empty glass. I was too content to be annoyed he was rushing me through my Chardonnay, which I finished in record time.

'Okay, I'm ready,' I announced a bit tipsily, my body pleasantly languid. I was so relaxed, in fact, that I appreciated the possessive grip of his hand on my arm helping me up as I slipped my purse strap over my other shoulder. We walked back into the hotel, the first floor of which consists of a small, highly expensive mall, and the bathrooms he was apparently leading me towards. 'I'll wait for you out here,' I said, but he kept firm hold of my arm as though he hadn't heard me. I only realized he was heading for the private phone booths directly beneath the stairs when he opened the door to one, at which point I opened my mouth to tell him he could use my cell-phone. Then how obvious that was clued me into the fact he had no intention of calling anyone as he directed me into the small space ahead of him. Stunned by this development (which I suppose I should have seen coming) and trying to make room for both of us in the cramped quarters, I dropped onto the bench facing him as he closed the door behind us.

'Eric!' I protested as he snatched the purse off my lap, and carelessly crammed it between the phone and the wall behind him. 'What are you doing?' I asked even though he was obviously unzipping his jeans directly in front of my face. 'Oh, my God,' I said as he shoved his underwear down with one hand and pulled his erection out with the other. It was no wonder his cock had felt so good when he was ramming into me from behind yesterday; his erect penis was so big, I wasn't able to take it in just with my eyes; I had to use my mouth to fully absorb its reality. Only when I felt the god-like hard-on pressing down on my tongue and against the roof of my mouth, completely filling my orifice, was I convinced it was very real indeed.

'Mm, yes...' he said, swiftly running the fingers of both hands through my hair to keep it out of my face, 'I see you like your little appetizer.'

I had to appreciate his sense of humor almost as much as his dream dick, yet although it filled my mouth it left the rest of me feeling strangely empty and anticipating my dinner date with Gerald tomorrow night even more intensely.

'That's right, suck my cock like a good girl... that's it, you can handle it, baby, just relax...'

I moaned half with excitement half in protest as he took control of my head. I planted my hands on his rock-hard denim thighs to brace myself, and also to be prepared to push him away if the exercise of swallowing the full length of his erection became too much for me. It seemed he was determined to push himself all the way down into my throat, and I was aching to give him what he wanted simplybecause it was an honor to have such a magnificent cock in my mouth. In the back of my mind, I told myself deep-throating was a skill any man would appreciate, including Gerald, and this was very good practice for pleasing him in the future.

'Oh, Ariana…' Eric slowly caressed his head with my throat over and over again, his hips unconsciously picking up speed as his pleasure intensified.

My eyes closing from the effort I was making to control my gag reflex, I moaned again, this time as a warning I couldn't take his selfish strokes much longer, mysteriously gratifying as they were. It was an immense relief when he slipped out of my mouth and let me catch my breath as I looked up at him.

He caressed my cheek. 'I think I need to fuck you again, Ariana.'

I bit my lip, wanting to protest, but I was unable to do so in the face of his erection. My pussy didn't care what my heart thought, it was juicing hungrily for that beautiful cock.

'Get up,' he commanded.

I obeyed, and he took my place on the bench. 'Come here,' he said.

'No.' I finally protested. I had no desire to ride him, which would mean facing him and having to look down into his eyes. 'I like it from behind,' I explained, lifting my dress up around my hips as I turned towards the phone and braced myself on it. I closed me eyes again in anticipation as he impatiently yanked my panties down to my knees. This time when he penetrated me the experience was even more devastatingly pleasurable as I was able to picture the length and girth of the rigid penis slipping up between my sex lips into my pussy. I cried out from the breathtaking fulfillment as he swiftly stabbed me with his full length.

'Quiet,' he whispered.

Somehow, I limited myself to strangled gasps of almost unbearable ecstasy as he plunged the full length of his erection in and out of my body with such fierce energy the intensity of the sensation killed my ability to think about anything or anyone else. Once again his thrusts propelled my senses to a transcendent place outside time and space, and his beating had begun to feel gloriously endless when he abruptly pulled out of me, leaving me feeling utterly bereft. I was too weak to resist as he turned me around. There was no need for him to tell me to sit down; my knees buckled and left me no choice.

'I'm going to come all over your face,' he warned. 'Close your eyes and open your mouth for me... oh, yes, that's it... I'm going to jack off all over your beautiful face... oh, yes!'

I accepted the hot baptism of his spunk over my features reluctantly but placidly, my eyelashes flickering as his pleasure rained down on my lips and cheeks.

When he was finished pumping himself dry, he asked matter-of-factly, 'Do you have a tissue in your purse?'

'Yes,' I replied, and waited until he handed it to me, and I wiped my face clean of his cum before opening my eyes.

He pulled me gently up into his arms. 'You're not leaving Miami,' he said firmly.

I sighed.

CHAPTER SIX

Personally, I feel that eating dinner slowly and appreciatively is part of how much I sensually enjoy my existence and savor its emotionally delicious mystery. I had told Eric I was having dinner with relatives that night even though he could easily have realized I was lying; it's common knowledge Cubans and other Hispanics eat their main meal in the afternoon. It seems to work for them, and many nutritionists recommend this eating regimen; nevertheless, I prefer to indulge myself in the evening when I'm no longer making an effort to be creative and productive, and I can fully relax while mentally digesting the fruit of my day's labors. I can't understand people who say it's not worth the effort to cook only for themselves. In my fervent opinion there's no one better worth cooking for than myself. If someone else also reaps the rewards of my passion and talent, so much the better, but it seems to me that being alone and not loving all your meals is only compounding one evil with another. I fully intended to treat myself to a nice dinner.

She sat with me in the kitchen drinking a cup of hot-chocolate while I indulged in another glass of Chardonnay, accompanied by some of my Tofu Spinach Artichoke Dip with corn chips. Eric's little appetizer, combined with walking to and from the hotel, had further stimulated my already healthy appetite. I'm blessed with a good metabolism, but I believe one of the reasons my body burns fat and calories so efficiently is because I keep it happy by never starving it or subjecting it to painfully limited food groups. I've always thought of my body as the horse my soul is riding through life, and I feel it's important to have a firm but loving relationship with it, an important part of which is always carefully listening to what it tells me about my habits and lifestyle.

Rosa watched me wolfing down the small bowl of dip with a slight frown knitting the fine skin between her light-brown eyebrows. She wasn't overweight, but she was plump – nicely rounded all over was how I affectionately saw her. 'How can you eat so much and not gain a pound?' she demanded wistfully, the question rhetorical; she asked me that every time I visited. 'That dip is very good,' she admitted.

'You tried some?' I asked happily. It never fails to please me when someone approves of one of my recipes.

'Yes, I had some before you came home, just a little. Are you sure that's made with tofu and Soy Parmesan?'

I laughed. 'Yes, I'm sure, I made it myself this afternoon.'

'Hmm.' Lover of all things purely Italian, it was difficult for her to admit liking anything containing Soy Parmesan.

Having savored my sweet secret long enough, I finally announced, 'Gerald is coming over for dinner tomorrow night, so you'll get to meet him.'

'Hmm!' She sipped her hot chocolate before remarking, her voice dripping with disapproval. 'And that's why you met someone else for drinks tonight? You've only been in Miami one day and you're already seeing two men!'

I grinned smugly as I rose to put the empty bowl in the sink and begin preparing my meal. 'I'm not really seeing Eric,' I pointed out, opening the refrigerator.

'Oh, weren't you just with him?'

For an instant, I lost my appetite for food remembering the hot wordless way my body had communicated with Eric's in that phone booth. 'Yes, I was,' I admitted, assembling the ingredients I needed on the counter. 'But it's just lust; I don't really care for him.'

'Lost? Who is lost?'

'Mami, you're so cute. Lost in lust...' I muttered, and sobered up somewhat. Eric, understandably, thought we were involved; he believed I planned on seeing (fucking) him again, and so far, the track record proved that when we were together I did, indeed, become lost in lust, and I could not afford to be, not when I was falling in love with someone else. I could no longer use the excuse that I had had sex with Eric before my date with Gerald (that had been true yesterday but not this evening) and part of me was thoroughly ashamed of (as well as a bit frightened by) my uncharacteristically wanton behavior. I hadn't been lying when I told Eric in that dingy little break room that I'd never done anything like that before. I could only conclude the death of my most recent relationship, compounded by my great aunt's death and burial, had affected me more deeply than I had realized. Things were happening fast, and even though I was consciously behind the wheel, so to speak, I didn't feel completely in control; my behavior kept slipping wickedly... my body kept crashing into Eric's head-on even though Gerald was the ideal destination chosen by my heart and soul...

'And why am I so cute?' My mother's mockingly stern tone roused me from my reverie. 'Who is lost?' she asked again.

'I think maybe I am,' I replied soberly. Fortunately just then the phone rang and she literally leapt out of her chair and ran into her bedroom to answer it. Apparently, she was expecting an important call, and my suspicion was confirmed when she failed to return, but I was too preoccupied with myself and how dangerously exciting my life had become since I arrived in Miami to wonder about hers. Instead, I soothed my turbulent thoughts and feelings with the sensually engaging task of preparing myself a nice dinner. I had recently discovered the pleasures of the other white meat, Pork, and had come to rely on it as much as on boneless skinless chicken breasts as part of my relatively healthful diet.

Forget thin dry pork chops, thick lean pork loin steaks will make you realize just how delicious pork can be when properly cut and prepared. As with boneless-skinless chicken breasts, the only danger here is how dangerously easy it is to overcook the chops so they come out dry and tough, not what you want. An important secret to achieving succulent results with low-fat meat is to first sear it in a frying pan – I use Extra Virgin Olive Oil – in order to seal in the juices while it bakes or broils. Once you know that, you can enjoy discovering the pleasures of Pork. You'll want to eat it just for the flavor not because it's low-fat.

ROSEMARY BAKED PORK LOIN CHOPS

Two thick (approximately two inches) Boneless Pork Loin Steaks
Sea Salt, to taste
Freshly Ground Black Pepper (don't be shy)
2 tsp Minced Garlic
2 Tbls Rosemary Infused Olive Oil*
Organic Chicken Broth
1/2 cup White Wine

Turn on the Broiler and heat the Rosemary Oil on high

while you season the Pork steaks, then sear them nicely on both sides before transferring them to a small glass or ceramic baking pan into which you've poured a shallow pool of White Wine and a little Chicken Broth. Whatever you do, don't use non-stick cookware for this recipe. (You can actually refrigerate the steaks at this point for a while, which I did once and discovered that sitting seared in the white wine made them amazingly tender.)

Broil the pork chops for approximately twenty minutes (I'm sure you've heard it before that oven and micro-wave temperatures vary) turn them over (use a tong if possible; piercing the steaks with a fork will permit vital juices to escape) baste them with the Chicken Broth-Wine mixture, adding a bit more Wine to the pan if necessary. Continue broiling the steaks until they're done, approximately ten more minutes.**

When you've determined the steaks are nearly done (absolutely never cook meat until it's completely done as the internal temperature rises at least five degrees after you remove it from the heat) take the pan out of the oven and cover it with tin foil for about five minutes to help release those precious inner juices. Finally, use the tongs to place each steak on a plate and pour the pan sauce equally over each one. The sauce will thicken slightly upon standing.

*You can use finely minced fresh rosemary if you can't find rosemary-infused olive oil or don't want to make the investment since it's a touch expensive, but it lasts a long time and the flavor is incomparable.

**This is the tricky part. I don't know what your oven is like or how thick the steaks you bought are, which is why I strongly recommend investing in an Instant Read Meat Thermometer that enables you to monitor the internal temperature of meat and poultry without slicing it open and releasing juices you want to remain sealed inside so the results are deliciously succulent. An Instant Read Thermometer takes all the mysterious fear out of cooking meats and is well worth the initial cost for all the confidence and pleasure it will give you. However, be advised that the "done" temperatures on many models are at least five to ten degrees exaggerated, erring on the side of caution, so after you've become familiar with your thermometer's eccentricities, use your own judgment, please.

CUBAN ROAST PORK

1 5-6 pound Boneless Pork Loin
Sea Salt
Freshly ground Black Pepper

Combine in a medium-sized mixing bowl:

4 -5 tsp Minced Garlic
1/2 tsp Dried Oregano
1/2 tsp Ground Cumin
1/4 cup Rum (or1 cup Dry Red or White Wine)
1/2 cup Orange Juice
1/4 Cup Lime Juice
3 Tbls Extra Virgin Olive Oil

Season the roast with the Sea Salt and freshly ground Black Pepper, slip it into a large plastic bag, and pour the marinade over it. Seal the bag and refrigerate for at least three hours or overnight, occasionally turning the roast over to evenly distribute the spices.

Preheat the oven to 325°, place the roast in a shallow roasting pan, and pour half the marinade over it. Cook for 2–2 1/2 hours, pouring the remaining marinade over the roast after about an hour-and-a-half. If the sauce begins to dry out, add a little water or chicken broth. The internal temperature should read 160°-165° when you remove the roast from the oven and cover it with tinfoil for 5-10 minutes to release more of its delicious juices. Carve the roast into 1/2 inch slices, pour the sauce over them (as well as in separate dipping saucers if you like) and serve.

Slices of left-over Cuban Roast Pork can be frozen in plastic bags for months and used to make Cuban Sandwiches.

CUBAN SANDWICHES

Cuban Bread (sliced in half lengthwise)
Light Safflower Mayonnaise (or whichever mayonnaise you prefer)
Dijon Mustard
Slices of Swiss Cheese
Slices of Sweet Ham (sweet Serrano ham if you can get it)
Left-over slices of Cuban Roast Pork
Dill Pickle Slices (the gourmet refrigerated kind, please)

Assemble your sandwiches in the order the ingredients are listed above, ending with the pickle slices, place on an electric grill, and flatten them as much as possible while the bread toasts and the cheese melts. Cut in half on the diagonal and serve at once. You can make them as thick or as thin as you desire. (If you don't have an electric grill or a sandwich press, use a large heavy frying pan to flatten the sandwiches, and then heat them uncovered in the oven.)

* * *

I lay awake in bed until late that night feeling increasingly guilty, restless and nervous. And yet that wasn't all I was feeling... I like to keep my pussy smoothly shaved, and as I lay on my back comfortably propped up against two feather pillows, my right hand just seemed to naturally find its way between my thighs to finger the pleasantly tender folds of my labia as thoughts flowed through my mind in mysterious high tide. Ever since my plane flew over the ocean and landed in Miami I had been flooded with feelings and desires threatening to drown my self control... in fact, I had gone under twice already with that beautiful Viking...

I closed my eyes as my fingertips brushed my clitoris and a pleasure subtle as butterfly wings brushing my nerve-endings suffused my sex, so that I scarcely noticed my thighs spreading open a little more against the soft mattress. I always sleep naked, even in the dead of winter up in Boston; I hate even the slight restriction of a cotton t-shirt becoming tangled around my torso as I toss and turn, buffeted by one dream after another. I never have a problem falling asleep, but I wake up dozens of times every night, which is perhaps one reason why I seem to remember all my dreams – vivid adventures in full living color involving places I've never been before and people I've never met. More than once I've been disappointed to wake up beneath my feather comforter when only an instant before I had been flying over the stunningly beautiful landscape of another planet, for instance. Flying in dreams is an intensely erotic experience for me; gravity ceases to pin me down and instead becomes my partner in an elemental dance, lifting me up and supporting me as I move gracefully and sensually in whichever way I desire. Whatever clothes I'm wearing in the dream invariably get stripped off as I soar towards the earth's atmosphere, until the exquisite moment when it's time to swiftly and deliberately begin falling, and I am increasingly aroused as the violent moment of contact approaches with whatever lies below me...

I caressed my clitoris with more energy, breathlessly amazed my real life had become almost as exciting as one of my flying dreams. The thought turned me on that I was daring to rise above the gravity of my usual reasonable self control and surrendering to impulses and sensations I would never have dared let myself fall into before. Stroking my clitoris with increasing fervor, I closed my eyes as the nerve-endings between my thighs glimpsed a climax glowing on their horizon... there was danger in this wildly erotic dream I was living in south Florida... I was behaving recklessly by fucking one man while falling in love with another...

An orgasm suddenly crashed between my legs and surged up through my body in a searing flash of pure pleasure. Thinking about seeing Gerald and remembering my hot encounters with Eric effortlessly plugged my body into a higher voltage of ecstasy than I had ever experienced before masturbating. Afterwards, I was relaxed and content for a few moments, during which I almost drifted off to sleep, but I didn't quite manage to escape into dreamland before thoughts started marching through my brain again as emotions warred with each other inside me.

Mami had been on the phone for a long time, and when she emerged from her bedroom the quality of her smile had told me more than I wanted to know; I was having a hard enough time dealing with my own burgeoning love life. Her hot-chocolate was ice-cold by the time she rejoined me in the kitchen, and my dinner was almost ready. Our eyes met, held for a significant moment, and I was relieved when I felt us both silently agree not to talk about her phone call yet. Sometimes my mother and I can communicate without words, so already I knew she had been on the phone with a man and that it was serious between them. I also knew that was all she wanted me to know for the moment, which was fine with me. But now, lying alone in the dark in my old bedroom, I couldn't help wondering who the man was as a childishly selfish part of me resented him for usurping some of my mother's love and attention. I excused my self-indulgence since I was sleeping in the bedroom where I grew up, and like a seashell it echoed hauntingly in the dark with the ever-changing currents of all the feelings and perceptions that had flowed through me through the years as I developed into the woman I was. And, apparently, I was transforming into yet another woman capable of doing things I never would have believed myself capable of only two days ago...

I deliberately turned my mind to the less complicated matter of the dinner I planned to prepare tomorrow evening for Gerald, and for a while I succeeded in entertaining myself trying to decide on what recipe to use for the precious filet mignon steaks I had splurged on that morning, and considering just the right side dishes to accompany them. But then the insidious possibility that I was avoiding larger issues and hungers in my life by once again concentrating on food ruined the simple pleasure I was taking in menu planning. I wondered if I was increasingly obsessed with food and nutrition because I was using culinary passion to suppress the pain I would otherwise be feeling over yet another failed relationship; however, I immediately dismissed the guilty suspicion. Breaking up with my last lover had definitely been the best thing to do, and the presence of Gerald in my life was only further proof I was on the right track. If only I hadn't met Eric… yet wishing away two such fulfilling sexual experiences struck me as a guilty anorexia of the soul: good girls have to keep their transgressions just a little more slender, we're not allowed to enjoy really sinfully good things that are supposedly bad for us somehow. Of course I didn't regret meeting Eric or how unbelievably good it had felt both times he fucked me from behind. It was not in my nature to regret the delicious effort of sucking him down and the dangerous thrill of being roughly possessed in a public place no matter what my Catholic upbringing said in the back of my head. There was no denying, however, that this out of work police officer complicated matters, and prone as I was to symbolically analyzing all the events in my life, the fact that he had fashioned a whole key for me from the broken one in my hand was too significant to ignore. Of course, I could easily be confusing the messenger with the message – that I had truly met my soul mate at last. Gerald had entered my life first, and my heart told me he was the long-awaited key to my future and happiness, not the Viking look-alike who had effort-lessly burned away my proper self control with his irresistible self confidence. I couldn't help but worry I was breaking some kind of cosmic law by not telling Eric once and for all I couldn't see him again. My intuition (no doubt fueled by my religious upbringing) was sure I was committing a metaphysical crime by leading Eric on that endangered my possible relationship with Gerald. After tomorrow night (if dinner went as well as I hoped it would) I could no longer cheat on Gerald or on my deepest feelings by indulging my essentially superficial attraction to Eric. The sexy cop with the big beautiful cock was like junk food to my soul, and tempting and tasty as he was in the heat of sexual hunger, a relationship with him could not possibly sustain me. I had tasted something totally new to my emotional palette – hot sex with a complete stranger – but I couldn't live off this thrill forever. For one thing, Eric was no longer a stranger, he had given me a pair of gold earrings, and the way he had said, 'You're not leaving Miami' made me feel even more guilty about the way my heart had leapt at his words as I hoped he was right, but I was thinking about another man as I smiled up into his eyes.

* * *

Gerald slowly and lovingly caressed the female form lying sub-missively motionless beneath his kneading hands. He had been working on her since midnight last night and he was exhausted, but he was also very pleased with how she was coming. He had not been so inspired by a woman in a long time, and once again he picked up one of his instruments to gently insert it between her thighs, smoothing the delicate lips of her sex with it. Her legs were spread open just wide enough to expose the full lips of her labia, which had taken him hours to lovingly shape. She was his best work so far, but he couldn't let Ariana know about her rival for his affections, not yet. It might offend her how intimate he was being with her in his imagination. She might resent the liberty he was taking by imagining what her most private parts looked like and by daring to shape them for his own selfish pleasure. Better to keep his secret for now…

CHAPTER SEVEN

In the morning, I got up relatively early and went for a jog before the sun was too high in the sky and it got too hot to even think of running. Up in Boston, the weather permitting, I enjoyed running along the water in the North End. I never went very far; twenty to twenty-five minutes three days a week felt like a good enough work-out to me and was all my knees could handle. The nice thing about where I lived in Boston was how convenient and pleasant it was to walk places or to take the train; I didn't even own a car. I got exercise every day just running errands, and buying gourmet groceries in all the specialty food stores I was surrounded by. I even had my own personal butcher! If I moved back down to Miami, all that would change; I would need to buy a car and shop at major grocery stores. These were the rather depressing thoughts running through my head for the first five minutes as I jogged leisurely down the back streets around mami's house, then the endorphins started kicking in and my outlook became increasingly positive as I admired all the beautifully maintained tropical foliage, one of the things that makes Coral Gables so nice to live in. By the time I walked breathlessly back into the house, I was feeling pleasantly relaxed and excited about what the future might bring.

After a long hot shower, I towel-dried my hair, then I slipped into a sleeveless cotton house dress and black leather flip-flops before setting off to the kitchen to quickly bake muffins for breakfast.

FIBER-FEST PUMPKIN MUFFINS

3 1/2 Cups Whole Wheat Flour
2 tsp Cinnamon
1 tsp Powdered Ginger
1/2 tsp Nutmeg
1 tsp Salt
6 tsp Baking Powder
1/4 cup Brown Sugar
2 Eggs
1/4 Cup Canola Oil
1 1/2 Cups Soy Milk
2 Tbls Butter, melted
1 16 oz Can Pumpkin Puree
Cooking Spray

Pre-heat the oven to 400° and coat a 12-muffin tin with the Cooking Spray. In a large bowl, mix all the dry ingredients together. In another medium-sized bowl, beat the Eggs with the Canola Oil, then add the Soy Milk and the melted Butter. Combine the wet ingredients with the dry ingredients, and finally stir in the Pumpkin Puree. Divide the batter into 12 muffin tins, then dust the top of each one with some more Brown Sugar and Cinnamon. Bake for 25-30 minutes, until a knife inserted in the center of one muffin comes out relatively clean. These breakfast treats are low-fat and full of great-for-you fiber.

CORN BREAD

1 Cup Unbleached Enriched White Flour
1 Cup Corn Meal
4 Tbls Unrefined Sugar
4 tsp Baking Powder
1 tsp Salt
1 Egg
1 1/4 Cups Soy Milk
2 Tbls Butter, melted
1 Tbls Canola Oil
Cooking Spray

Pre-heat the oven to 350°. Combine all the dry ingredients in one bowl, then in another bowl beat the Egg with the melted Butter and the Canola Oil before stirring in the Soy Milk.

Lightly coat a bread pan with the Cooking Spray, pour in the batter, and bake for 30-40 minutes, until a knife inserted in the center of the loaf comes out relatively clean.

* * *

After what felt like an endless day, when Gerald finally walked through the door that night – casually but elegantly dressed in black slacks and a finely starched white button-down shirt – I knew it was a sight I wanted to experience for the rest of my life. It was mami who actually let him in; I saw him step into the living room from the vantage point of the kitchen from which I had quickly emerged when the doorbell rang, but then I deliberately paused on the threshold to enjoy the full effect of his presence in my childhood home. From a distance, I could appreciate even more how tall and slender he was except for his shoulders, which were breathtakingly broad. He looked over at me, and the quality of his smile made me feel as though his pleasure was the sun rising directly in my heart and illuminating my life for all the years to come. I am not exaggerating; that's exactly how the sight of him entering my living space made me feel, and I use a poetic metaphor because it's the only way to express the happiness that possessed me. I had eyes only for him, but a quick glance at mami told me she was quite favorably impressed by our guest's aura as well as by his physical appearance, because my intuitive mother never merely judges a book by its cover. I saw all the lines of her body subtly relax as she stepped aside to let him pass, and I sensed she had let down her defenses; she was willing to believe this might actually be the right man for me at last.

'Good evening, ladies,' he said in the deep, quiet voice that turned the marrow in my bones into a wonderful drug soothing away all worries and concerns. He smiled down at my mother for a polite instant before looking over at me again where I stood at the entrance to the kitchen, and the look in his eyes made the carpet beneath my high-heels feel treacherous as sand beneath the surf-like pounding of my heart. I somehow knew beyond a shadow of a doubt that I was looking at my soul mate miraculously standing in the living room where I once played with my Barbie dolls, and in response my heart was pounding the double beat of joy and disbelief.

'Good evening,' Rosa echoed. 'Oh my…' She glanced at me, and it was only then I noticed the extravagant bouquet of violet roses he was holding in his left hand. In his right hand was a slender brown bag obviously containing a bottle of wine.

'Hi!' I declared inanely, hurrying over to relieve him of his burdens, but mami had already taken possession of the flowers.

'These are beautiful,' she exclaimed, 'and such an unusual color.'

'It's my favorite color,' I reminded her, pleased that he was showing he remembered our conversation about all the different shades of violet visible in the desert. I felt it was important we always remembered everything we said to each other.

'Is it your favorite color, really?' she asked innocently. My mother loves me dearly, but she has never been able to remember details like my favorite color. 'Well, I'll go put them in water for you,' she offered possessively.

'I know that a rose by any other name would smell as sweet, but…' My date's eyes glinted with mischief as he grinned at me.

'Oh, sorry… Gerald, this is my mother, Rosa,' I introduced them, then added, 'Thank you' as I relieved him of the wine bottle.

'It's a great pleasure to meet you, Rosa.' He sounded perfectly sincere.

'Ariana, aren't you going to ask our guest to sit down and offer him a drink?'

'Yes mami.'

'Well then, what are you waiting for?' She also took the bottle from me. 'I'll put this on the table for dinner and be right back with these.' She walked away towards the kitchen still admiring the roses, and her wistful smile clearly told me she wished they were for her from another man.

'Come here.' The second she disappeared into the kitchen, Gerald's arms slipped around my waist and pulled me against him. I lifted my face up to his, breathlessly awaiting his kiss, but all he did was gaze down into my eyes with the softest of smiles on his lips. His mouth had pressed politely against mine last night just before we parted, but our tongues had not yet danced nakedly and intimately together.

'I'm so glad you're here,' I told him, and it was as if my arms had always been meant to rest around his neck.

'Then why aren't you smiling?' he teased, pressing my body even more firmly against his.

'Because… because I'm afraid,' I confessed, trying earnestly to convey a world of thoughts, and feelings and desires to him with my eyes staring up into his.

'Afraid of what, Ariana?' he asked gently, the smile fading from his lips like the sun vanishing behind the cloud of my stormy emotions.

'Of the way I already feel about you,' I admitted bluntly, forcing myself to slip out of his arms and take an objective step away from him.

To my infinite relief, he immediately pulled me towards him again. 'You should be happy about the way we feel,' he said sternly, and suddenly his tongue was dancing with mine in a way that made me forget everything else. I would have stood there clinging to him and kissing him until my mother returned if he had not shown more presence of mind and let go of me first.

* * *

This wine is quite nice,' Rosa admitted reluctantly, turning the bottle towards her where it sat in the middle of the dining room table so she could study the label. 'Constancia Cellars... I've never heard of it.'

'It's a South African vineyard,' Gerald informed her in his perpetually quiet, even voice.

'Hmm, a Cabernet-Shiraz blend... very nice,' she concluded, paying the wine, and the person who had bought it, a great compliment indeed by approving a non-Italian vintage.

I personally could have cared less where the wine came from. Normally grape varieties interest me very much, and I have my own personal affordable favorite wines I buy regularly, but that night I cared only about the man sitting at the head of the table. Mami had done a beautiful job setting it as I prepared dinner, and both the scene and the company were so perfect and beautiful I felt as though I had entered an alternate universe where people, objects and events all come together as they do in movies and in dreams to create truly fulfilling moments; moments you can savor even while looking forward to more mysteriously delicious ones in the future. At the same time I felt the pang of realizing what I had been missing; what lackluster, unsatisfying circumstances I had been forced to survive in before tasting real happiness and contentment. My first home-made dinner with Gerald was definitely an occasion worthy of the family's fine china and polished silverware; of the black wrought-iron candelabra crowned with the slender columns of six violent candles; and of the crystal stemware reflecting the natural, pulsing light.

'Ariana, this is the best filet mignon I've ever tasted,' Gerald told me without looking up from his plate as he sliced himself yet another bite of meat and thrust it with an endearing childish eagerness into his mouth.

His appetite, and his compliment, both pleased me immensely. As I mentioned, my brother (also a Boston resident, to my mother's chagrin) is a Vegan and I love him dearly, but I could never consider a relationship with a man who doesn't eat meat. Yet a man who only eats meat and doesn't enjoy seafood or many vegetables, for example (my last boyfriend) was also wrong for me. I had been looking for and (judging by the conversation so far) had at last found a man who was a true omnivore.

'Ariana is a wonderful cook,' my mother threw in proudly. 'The first thing she did yesterday was grocery shop and fill my kitchen with more food than it's seen in years!'

Gerald's smile deepened. 'I don't think my kitchen even remembers it ever was a kitchen.'

'He keeps books in his oven and toilet paper in his refrigerator,' I explained.

Rosa giggled, her cheeks attractively flushed from the wine. 'Well, you'll fix that!' she declared without thinking, yet the atmosphere at the table didn't become awkward or embarrassing as a result of her tipsy slip. In fact, the moment turned into one of those magic bubbles I knew would forever float happily in my memory as proof that not all dreams evaporate when Gerald casually replied, 'I hope so' before taking another sip of his wine. Mami and I glanced at each other then, both of us still not quite able to believe this man wasn't an illusion, and for a sticky sentimental instant our eyes and hearts melted together like candy with the sweet certainty he truly was real and going to give us both what we wanted. I wanted my soul mate, she wanted me to move back to Miami, and against all odds our desires were going to come together and be fulfilled, proving there was a God. Then suddenly I felt the parent inside Rosa force her true nature into becoming protectively skeptical for an awkward moment.

'I just realized, Gerald,' she said in the unnaturally tight voice of her assumed persona, 'that I don't know what you do for a living.'

The truth was I wanted to know myself, but I still felt like killing her for daring to grill him like that.

He calmly cleaned his plate before replying, even more quietly than he normally spoke, 'I'm an artist.'

'You're an artist?' Rosa exclaimed. 'That's wonderful! Are you a painter?'

I could tell he was surprised, almost stunned, by her response; her enthusiasm a disorienting bomb going off in place of the disapproving silence he had apparently come to expect from many people (not to mention a prospective in-law) since artists rarely make much money. 'No, I'm a sculptor,' he confessed, meeting my eyes, and in their dark depths I suddenly saw the piece we had been looking at in the gallery, the sculpture of a man and woman making love...

'You're a sculptor?' Rosa regarded him with awe. Not only did this strikingly handsome man possess Italian blood, his already special blood was obviously pure enough to contain the creative gene obsessed with beauty that in her opinion set Italians above all other mortals.

'Was that your piece in the gallery?' I exclaimed. 'It was, wasn't it?' I went on excitedly before he could reply. 'That's why you looked at me that way when I said it was the only thing I'd seen all night I really liked.'

'A gallery here in the Gables is showing your work?' Rosa gasped.

He shrugged. 'The owner's a friend of mine,' he said humbly, looking a little uncomfortable.

'That's wonderful, I must see it. Which gallery is it in?'

'We can talk about that later, mami,' I said quickly, sensing and respecting his modesty, 'right now it's time for dessert.'

He smiled at me. 'That was an incredible meal, Ariana, and very filling; I don't think I can eat another bite.'

'I normally don't have dessert either, but tonight's a special occasion.'

'Yes, it is,' he agreed. 'Okay, you talked me into it.'

'I didn't make it; it's just chocolate ice cream and whipped cream.'

'Wonderful.' He pushed his chair back and made as if to pick up his plate and help clean up.

'You sit down at once, young man!' Rosa commanded with all the authority her soft golden plumpness could muster. 'You're our guest. I'll clear the table while Ariana brings out dessert, then I'll make us all some coffee.'

'Sounds wonderful, Rosa, thank you,' he said, but he was looking at me, and his smile tasted sweeter to my soul than any dessert ever could.

PAN-GRILLED SIRLOIN STEAKS

Coat two thick Sirloin Steaks generously with Extra Virgin Olive Oil to seal in the juices during cooking, brush with 2-3 tsp minced Garlic, season liberally with Sea Salt and freshly ground Black Pepper, then refrigerate until thirty minutes before you're ready to grill.

Heat a grill pan or preferably an electric grill* on high until hot, coat lightly with Cooking Spray and add the steaks, making sure to catch the juices as they flow out during cooking if using en electric grill.

Turn the steaks once after about five minutes, cook another three minutes or so (it all depends on how thick your steaks are) then begin testing for doneness, preferably by inserting an instant read thermometer into the thickest part of one steak. Remove the steaks from the grill when they're ten degrees below the required temperature of however you like your meat cooked, and cover them with tinfoil for about five minutes. The steaks will finish cooking while releasing their delicious juices. (The cooking time given here is for medium-rare or a nice pink center.)

Meanwhile, pour some White or Red Wine into the grill pan and scrape off the browned bits with a wooden spoon. (If using an electric grill, pour the wine onto the grill so it flows into the juices that have run off the grill during cooking, then once or twice pour this sauce over the grill, catching it in a separate container. Uncover the steaks and pour the sauce over them. By now they'll be sitting in a pool of their own juices. Serve at once.

*I highly recommend investing twenty-five dollars or so in a small electric grill, which is great for making sandwiches as well.

PAN-GRILLED FILET MIGNONS

4 Filet Mignon Steaks, about 1 1/2 pounds total
Extra Virgin Olive Oil
Sea Salt
Freshly Ground Black Pepper

Combine:
1 1/2 tsp Minced Garlic
1 1/2 Tbls Dijon Mustard
1 1/2 Tbls Green Peppercorns, slightly crushed with a knife

White Wine for deglazing

Brush the steaks with the Olive Oil, season with Salt and Pepper, then spoon a thin layer of the Garlic, Mustard and the Peppercorn mixture onto both sides of each steak.

Grill for about 3 minutes on each side (capturing any juices that escape if using an electric grill) then remove the steaks from the grill and tent them beneath tinfoil to finish cooking and release the internal juices. Meanwhile, deglaze the grill with White Wine (see previous recipe) and pour the sauce over the steaks.

LOADED BAKED POTATOES

2 Large Baking Potatoes
Extra Virgin Olive Oil
Sea Salt
Freshly Ground Black Pepper
Light Sour Cream
Extra Sharp Cheddar Cheese, grated
Real Bacon Bits (optional)

I always thought I had to wrap my potatoes in tinfoil to bake them, but I could not have been more wrong. The result was a soggy skin and a boring interior with a slightly unpleasant smoky flavor and a texture that was somehow wrong. I've been devouring cookbooks for years (no pun intended) and one day I read somewhere that potatoes should never be baked in foil. I embraced the unorthodox idea, and I have since come up with my version of the ideal baked potato.

Cover a small shallow oven pan with tin foil and preheat the oven to 425°. Wash the potatoes, pat them dry, then with a fork pierce the skin three to four times on each side. Place the potatoes on the foil and drizzle a small amount of Extra Virgin Olive Oil over each one, rubbing it into the skin with your fingertips. Finally, season them with Sea Salt and slip them into the oven to bake for a full hour-and-a-half. Yes, that's right, I said bake them for at least ninety minutes. The longer the potatoes stay in the oven, the crispier their skin will get and the fluffier their insides will be.

Remove the potatoes from the oven and allow them to cool somewhat before taking a sharp knife and gauging out a good portion of the insides, cutting around the edges almost down to the center to form a bowl-shape, reserving the lid. Season both halves of each potato with Sea Salt and freshly ground Black Pepper. Spoon some light Sour Cream onto them, cover them with the grated Cheddar Cheese and, if desired, sprinkle them with real bacon bits. Place the potato halves back in a 350° degree oven and heat them until the cheese is nicely melted. You may then cover each potato with its seasoned top or serve them separately.

ROASTED ROSEMARY POTATOES

1 lb Small White Potatoes
1 Tbls Rosemary Olive Oil
Sea Salt, to taste
Freshly Ground Black Pepper, to taste

Preheat the oven to 425°. Wash the Potatoes, pat them dry, then place them on a non-stick cookie sheet. Drizzle them with the Rosemary infused Olive Oil and toss them around to coat each piece with as much of the oil as possible. Season them with the Sea Salt and freshly ground Black Pepper and then bake them for approximately forty-five minutes, tossing them once or twice during cooking so all sides get nicely browned. Serve at once.

CHAPTER EIGHT

Gerald stayed late, long after Rosa had tactfully gone to bed. We sat on the cream-colored couch as close together as possible, talking and talking like old friends who haven't seen each other in centuries. We had opened another bottle from my mother's rack, and the wine flowed as freely as our thoughts and feelings mingling without any predetermined direction; we talked about everything and anything that came into our minds, only occasionally interrupting our conversation to kiss silently and lingeringly, the crystal glasses in our hands an exquisite torment since they made it impossible for us to embrace. We could easily have set our glasses down on the coffee table, but I deliberately kept mine in hand because I was afraid of going too far too fast with this very special man, and I wanted to do everything right with him. Of course, I had no idea what the proper metaphysical procedure was for soul mates to follow when they were at last fortunate enough to actually meet each other.

According to social tradition, it was healthy to wait at least a little while before becoming physically intimate with a prospective life-long mate, so I was perversely determined not to sleep with him right away. Naturally, my body paid absolutely no attention to this abstract moral mandate; it was ready to get naked with him right then and there, but my paranoid mind vetoed the evidence of all my senses (including my sixth sense) and stubbornly held its ground. I explained to him how I felt – that we should wait at least another night or two before we made love – and he graciously aided me in my struggle to resist him by also holding on to his wine glass instead of doing devastating things to me with his hand. It was distracting enough just having the delicious pressure of his arm draped over my shoulders, not to mention the sweet distraction of his free hand every now and then stroking my hair as we spoke. Not for one second did I consider my prudish behavior now paradoxical in light of how I had recently behaved with a complete stranger. I had had sex with Eric, that was all, and what I wanted from Gerald was much more. When Gerald and I came together, I knew it would be an intense experience bringing all levels of my being into play; therefore, it was an event I had to brace myself for precisely because its metaphysical explosiveness could seriously hurt me if I stepped blithely into it like an emotional landmine. When this man entered my body it would mean a lot to me, and part of me enjoyed savoring the anticipation even as my free hand suddenly reached down and lightly caressed the hard-on buried inside his pants.

'I'm sorry,' I said, 'I just couldn't resist.'

He placed his own free hand over mine. 'That's all right, I like it there.'

'I don't want to tease you…'

'You're not teasing me, Ariana. I understand your concerns, and I'm perfectly willing to wait.'

'I know it seems silly…'

'I could never consider anything you wanted silly.'

'I've thought a lot about sex.'

He laughed softly. 'So have I.'

'No, I'm serious, I–'

'So am I.'

I sighed. 'I really don't think there's such a thing as making love, Gerald.'

He was silent for a moment. 'What do you mean?' he asked.

'I mean there's no such thing as love-making when you're having sex, because sex is sex, and sex is inherently violent, you know; penetration is not a gentle act. I mean, foreplay can sometimes be tender, kissing and caressing, and all that, but sex itself is never tender; if it is, it's impotent and boring.' I paused in an effort to find the right words for how I felt.

'Go on…'

'I believe love-making relates to every other aspect of a couple's life,' I continued, encouraged by his profound attention. 'When a man and a woman truly love each other, everything they do for each other is making love – holding each other at night, cuddling up together to watch a movie, one of them cooking for the other, listening to each other's thoughts and feelings about everything every day for the rest of their lives knowing they'll always be there for each other sharing everything together – all that is love-making, but when they have sex, they're having sex, not making love. Sex is its own mysterious dimension.'

'And you don't think sex is more special between two people who love each other, Ariana?'

'Oh yes, of course I do,' I assured him fervently, looking up into his eyes for an instant before staring off into space again as though reading cosmic cue cards helping me express myself. 'Sex is much more intense between two people who love each other because it's mysteriously charged by their love and deepened by their soulful connection to each other, but it isn't necessarily only an expression of their love for each other, although obviously it can be; most of the time it's still purely sex.' I sighed again. 'I really don't know how to express it. I've been reading articles about how pervasive pornography is becoming in our society, not just through XXX films now but also through computers and the internet. So many couples get divorced when the woman finds out her husband is secretly into pornography. They feel betrayed, like they're not good enough for him, and I think they're wrong. I think they don't understand that love and sex can be two totally different things, not just in a man's psyche but in reality. These women believe in the myth of love-making in relation to sex, but making love is mainly about the life you build with someone and how much your souls care especially for each other... I went to a strip club with one of my ex-boyfriends once,' I confessed, 'and afterwards when we went home I felt completely empowered, not in the least degraded. It was as if my body was imbued with the flesh of all those other women... as if my body was all women's bodies and he was passionately worshipping the universal power of my sex through my own personal unique embodiment of it. I think women need to realize that love and sex are two different forces, and that how much a man truly loves them has nothing to do with his need for pure sex. I mean it's ridiculous and damaging to think less of men for obeying a metaphysical principle, isn't it? Women really need to realize they have the power to give the man they love everything he desires and to fulfill their own secret fantasies by not always confusing love-making with sex; by willingly merging their flesh with the flesh of all other women in a sacred, positive interpretation of what feminists consider a degrading objectification of the female body. A man and a woman who truly love each other should think of sex as a safari they enjoy going on together – it's unpredictable, it's wild, it can be dangerous and even violent, but ultimately it's a fun adventure that brings their souls closer together instead of tearing them apart... Am I making any sense at all?'

'Ariana, you make more sense than anyone I've ever met.' He kissed the top of my head. 'But now I think I'd better leave because I'm getting so turned on I won't be able to walk soon.'

'Oh, please don't go yet. You haven't finished your wine.'

His smile deepened as he stared into my eyes. 'You're right, I haven't finished my wine,' he agreed, but then he took my glass from me and set it down along with his on the coffee table. 'That's not why I'm staying though.' He took my hand and helped me up off the couch. 'Where's your bedroom?'

'But...'

'Don't worry, I respect your desire to wait, and this isn't the right place anyway.' He glanced in the direction of Rosa's bedroom. 'All I want is to see you naked.' He suddenly grabbed me by the hips and pulled me to him. 'I need to see you naked, Ariana, so I'm going to undress you, then tuck you in.'

'But...'

He let go of me. 'Go brush your teeth and wash up.' He sank gracefully down onto the couch again. 'I'll finish my wine while you get ready for bed like a good girl.' The soft smile never left his lips but his dark eyes were intensely serious; inarguably sober even as he retrieved his wine glass and took a patient sip while I just stood there. 'Is something wrong, Ariana? You're not saying that you don't you trust me to respect your wishes, are you?'

His mild tone did not fool me; he was testing the depth, sincerity and strength of my purported feelings for him, and the way he challenged me made me so happy, I was speechless for a crucial moment that caused him to misinterpret my silence.

'Should I leave?' he asked so softy his voice might have been the whisper of my own blood beating through my heart in those crossover moments I would remember forever.

'No, please don't go, Gerald, I… I trust you, I just don't… I just don't trust myself. I mean, how can I be naked in front of you and not–'

'I already told you nothing is going to happen tonight, Ariana,' he spoke kindly but firmly, 'so don't worry, you can be as weak as you like.' He paused to sip his wine. 'I won't let you fall.'

'Oh God…' I glanced up at the ceiling before once again meeting the eyes of the man who already had more power over me than any abstract idea of divinity ever would. 'All right,' I said. 'I'll be right back, I'm just going to brush my teeth.'

'I'll be here. Don't rush. I want you to do everything you would normally do before going to bed.'

'Everything? Even wash my face and take off my make-up?'

'Yes.' He arched a dark eyebrow as though how much I was questioning him was making him even more incredulous than I felt. 'Everything, Ariana.'

I sighed, 'Okay!' and turned away.

Once in the bathroom, I flicked on the light and quickly closed the door behind me. Shining irises the color of tiger's eyes looked back at me above flushed cheeks and a radiant smile of disbelief. Sometimes how beautiful I am surprises me, but that night it truly stunned me, and I realized it was because I was seeing myself though Gerald's eyes. His perception of me felt so amazingly wonderful, it was a few moments before I could focus enough to pick up my toothbrush, and perform the mechanical task of cleaning my teeth. Then I washed off my make-up with an exfoliating facial cleanser, patted my skin dry with a soft towel, and finished off with a nocturnal moisturizing cream I smoothed dreamily into my cheeks and neck. Finally, I brushed out my hair and, bracing myself, walked back out into the living room almost wishing he had left while I still had all my defenses intact.

He stood up when he saw me, abandoning his empty glass. 'Where's your bedroom?' he asked again.

All my nerves stood up on end like a cat's back because there was no getting away from it; it was inevitable, I was going to sleep with him tonight, all my moral resolutions be damned. 'Over there.' I indicated the side of the house opposite from the one my mother occupied.

'Good.' He slipped my hand into his again, and I obediently led him to the bedroom in which I had slept since I was a baby until I left home in my early twenties.

The room was absolutely dark, protected from the penetrating glare of streetlights by the lush tropical foliage growing in front of both windows. There was no way in hell I was going to turn on the overhead light. I said, 'Just a minute' and instinctively found my way to a lamp on the nightstand. I switched it on, and my breath caught as I turned around in time to see him closing the door behind us. Suddenly, I couldn't believe he was there and was real. I had to make an effort not to sink down onto the bed behind me as my knees nearly buckled beneath a profound rush of mingled relief and disbelief. He looked so tall and elegant in his black pants and white shirt almost like a businessman but much sexier; the top three buttons of his shirt were undone, and at some point during the evening he had rolled the long sleeves casually up to his elbows. He gazed curiously around my old bedroom, his eyes and smile lingering on my beloved collection of all-time favorite Barbie dolls – thirteen of them standing, sitting and reclining on a table in the corner.

'I never played with baby dolls,' I informed him proudly.

His expression did not change as he looked from my dolls back to me. 'Take off your dress,' he said.

I almost felt made of plastic myself and needing his willpower just to move my arms so I could obey him. I was wearing a simple red dress with spaghetti straps that clung gently to my bra-free breasts and to my hips, a style I find more flattering to my figure than the tight spandex look. The skirt fell to mid-thigh, showing off my long bare legs flatteringly balanced on red high-heeled sandals. After my shower that afternoon, I had made sure the paint on my toenails was also the exact same shade of red as my shoes and dress. The only contrast I had chosen was one he could not see yet – white cotton bikini panties.

'Would you like my help?' he teased when I failed to obey him, and took a threatening step towards me.

'No,' I said quickly, because if he touched me I was lost. I lifted the dress up over my head, and would have tossed it carelessly away if he hadn't reached out and taken it from me. He raised it to his face, inhaling the scent of my skin as he caressed the soft fabric. His smile had vanished, replaced by a contemplative look, and the sensual way the fabric draped over his hands made me aware of how long and strong his fingers were, and their firm, rounded ends looked as strangely sensitive as I knew they were slightly rough. Then at last he turned his eyes up from my lifeless frock and took in my naked body, completely exposed before him except for white bikini panties and red high-heels.

The crimson cloth seemed to faint at his feet clad in black shoes stepping silently across the carpet towards me. 'You're beautiful, Ariana.'

I had always known I possessed a nice figure, but the way he looked at me made me feel as though every part of my body was a work of art mysteriously fashioned in just the right way to please him. I had expected to feel shy and awkward as I held myself perfectly still, and was surprised that I didn't; it felt wonderfully natural to hold myself motionless as he studied me. There was just enough space between me and the bed for him to step behind me, and I caught my breath as his cool clothes brushed my warm bare flesh. I waited for him to touch me, but he didn't; he just looked me silently up and down from all angles. I remembered then – with the small part of my brain that could think about anything besides how much I wanted him to touch me – that he was a sculptor, a very good, a very talented, sculptor with a feel for how a man and a woman's bodies merged during sex...

I closed my eyes as he stepped in front of me again. I didn't understand how it was possible we weren't going to make love. I was so turned on by his scrutiny, so aroused by the lingering caress of his awareness, it seemed a crime to let him leave and to just go to sleep, as if I possibly could...

'I'd like to take your panties off for you, Ariana,' he said quietly, meeting my eyes. 'May I?'

'Yes,' I whispered.

The first touch of his fingers against my skin was literally electric from static build-up in the carpet. I gasped, and a flash of amusement softened his firm mouth for an instant as he gently hooked his thumbs into my panties, then slowly pulled them down as he sank to one knee before me, caressing my hips and the edges of my thighs and legs with his hands. I stepped out of them carefully, my equilibrium threatened by much more than high-heels.

'Mm!' Rising, he inhaled the intimate fragrance clinging to my delicate undergarment. 'You're wet, Ariana,' he accused mildly. 'Does it excite you to be looked at?'

'You're not being fair,' I replied helplessly. 'Of course I'm excited, how could I–'

'Relax,' he urged gently, and stepped right up to me so only a charged breath of air separated my painfully hard nipples from his soft shirt. 'I'm glad it excites you to be looked at naked.' He stroked the hair away from my face with both hands and the balls of his thumbs brushed my cheeks in a way that was both caressing and assessing. 'You're going to be doing a lot of modeling for me in the future, Ariana.'

'Oh, I would love that…'

'But now I just want you to be a good girl and lie back across the bed for me… just sit on the edge… that's right, and lie back.'

'But…' I protested even as my body languidly did as he requested. 'But you said…'

'Relax,' he repeated softly, 'I just want to see all of you.'

I closed my eyes as he spread my legs, then desperately clutched the comforter as I felt him kneel directly between them. The experience of his hands pushing open my thighs was so exquisite that resisting whatever he intended to do was inconceivable to me.

'Oh, yes,' he whispered.

I bit my lip thinking I should be embarrassed that he was studying my pussy so closely, yet I wasn't; however, I was very glad I had shaved earlier and that my sex was nice and smooth to the touch. 'Oh, no, Gerald,' I protested faintly, yet I didn't move a muscle to stop him, my willpower effortlessly undone by the sensation of his fingertip thrusting gently between the folds of my labia directly beneath where my clitoris huddled shyly beneath its hood, then slowly traveling down the length of my slit.

'It's all right, Ariana…'

He was reassuring me, but the sensation of his warm breath on the vulnerably open cleft in my flesh only deepened my desire for him almost painfully. I wanted his hard cock inside me and I wanted it now; it was stupid to wait, he was my soul mate, for Christ's sake. 'Please!' I begged ambiguously, meaning, 'Please take me!' and 'Please, don't…' all in one paradoxical breath. 'Oh, yes,' I moaned as his tongue suddenly licked its way up between my sex lips, then its energetic tip flickered just beneath my clitoris and roused it out from beneath its fleshy cover so swiftly and skillfully the intensity of the pleasure I felt dazed me. I told myself he was only licking my pussy; that we weren't fucking so he hadn't broken his promise, not really. 'Oh, my God…' His tongue possessed skills I had never dreamed of. I couldn't believe it; it wasn't possible that already I could feel myself starting to come. The skilled and fervent working of his tongue was showing my body the way to go, urging it to surrender to the sweet, hot bliss building up between my thighs in record time. 'Oh, Gerald… oh, my God!' My flesh could not distinguish between them, especially when he suddenly thrust one hard finger all the way up inside me, pointing out how deep and wet and open I was with such devastating effectiveness I immediately began climaxing. I arched my back and clung to the comforter for all I was worth as I silently rode the wave of a miraculously fast and powerful orgasm. When it was over – when my ecstasy had stopped rushing into his mouth like the flood from a broken dam, my clitoris glowing with something much more precious than the price of a pearl – I opened my eyes and raised my head off the bed to look at the man kneeling between my thighs. His eyes met mine over my naked body, and in that moment I was forced to face the unbelievable fact that I was already profoundly, inescapably in love with him. I was too weak, for a myriad of reasons, to move as he stood up.

'Now I can say good night,' he said.

I started to sit up.

'No, stay right there,' he commanded gently. 'I want to remember you just as you are now. Don't worry, I can let myself out.'

'But…' It took all the willpower I possessed to merely stare up at the ceiling when I so much wanted to look at him. 'When will

I see you again, Gerald?'

'Tomorrow, of course. Good night, Ariana.'

I relaxed, and turned my head so I could watch him as he walked away. 'Good night,' I called after him.

He opened the door. 'Sweet dreams,' he said, and closed the door quietly behind him.

CHAPTER NINE

I slept as peacefully as a well-loved baby all night long, waking only once to relieve myself of the wine I had imbibed, and in the morning I got up ready to deal with my familial responsibilities. I had behaved quite selfishly since I arrived in Miami; it was time to face my relatives. The social whirlwind surrounding my great aunt's funeral had died down by now, so mami and I planned to spend the afternoon with my grandfather to help him with the transition back to a normal life his sister would no longer be a part of. To that end, I spent most of the morning in the kitchen contentedly cooking. Abuelo subscribed to a local cantina that brought him his favorite Cuban dishes every night, and last time I saw him he appeared quite content with the food delivered to his home, a service taken advantage of by many elderly and disabled persons in Miami. However, whenever I saw him he made it clear there was nothing like 'Ani's home cooking'. He considered me to be the best cook the family had ever produced, and considering how many people the family tree boasted, and how many of them at least thought of themselves as superlative cooks, this was quite a compliment indeed. So I spent the morning roasting a whole chicken for him he could enjoy for two meals, tossing him up a large salad, since I knew fresh greens were lacking in his cantina dependent diet, and preparing his all-time favorite dish, Picadillo. I also made him a large batch of my Tofu Macaroni and Cheese, dividing it into separate containers for him. He could freeze them, then defrost individual portions in the microwave mami had bought him and taught him how to use (her stubbornness won out over his.)

It was my off day running, which was nice because I was already feeling wonderfully relaxed. Boston seemed as far away as it was old – a strangely dark and vague memory on the horizon of my thoughts despite the fact that I had left there only a few days ago. I wasn't making any conscious decision yet about moving back down to Florida, not because it was too soon but because I was afraid to tempt fate. All the signs pointed south to absolute sensual fulfillment and happiness, but part of me still couldn't quite trust how fast it was happening. I was keeping one cautious foot on my emotional break, just in case, even while savoring the scenery of absolute contentment emerging inside me, a temperamental landscape I was not at all accustomed to; I always had at least one little thing to feel blue about. But the morning after Gerald came to dinner everything felt different, as though gravity had become just a little bit lighter, just a little bit more dream-like. It would be a cliché (not to mention a physical impossibility in Miami) to say the sun shone more brightly that day, but that's what it felt like, as though the mysterious tarnish of doubt had been wiped clean from my perceptions, and for the first time since I was a little girl I believed, I knew, that dreams could come true.

While the chicken roasted, I slipped off my apron and wandered into my bedroom, where I idly picked up one of my Barbie dolls, smiling fondly at her. I was glad Gerald had seen them. I knew now he lived right here in the Gables. Amazingly enough, he and my mother had been neighbors for years. It almost hurt to think about the time I had wasted up North not knowing the man I had dreamed of all my life was right here at home, yet I knew it was foolish to regret anything I had done because it was all part of what I called the Magic Pattern – the web of circumstances surrounding me constantly being played like haunting strings by my feelings and events and other people to create the unique melody of my life… my cell phone rang.

I carelessly dropped the Barbie I was holding, and snatched up the little metal fragment of technology lying on one of my pillows where I had carefully laid it when I entered the room. Before that my phone had been resting on a black pot holder while I cooked, and before that it had reclined across a white towel in the bathroom as I showered. I had no intention of missing Gerald's call whenever or wherever it came.

'Hello, Ariana.'

My room darkened as the sun momentarily vanished behind a cloud. 'Hello, Eric.' I had succeeded in forgetting all about him or almost. The truth was I had simply filed his wild card in the very back of my mind hoping my silence would cause him to fold and that our little game would end so I could stop worrying about the gamble I had made fucking him. I was afraid the way I had cheated on my deeper feelings would cause me to lose everything I was hoping for now.

'You don't sound very happy to hear from me, Ariana.' His words were accusing but his tone was casual – a thin glove over the guilt he was trying to hit me with. He had insisted I give him my cell phone number before we parted at the Colonnade, and considering what I had just let him do to me in a public phone booth, it hadn't felt right to withhold a mere few numbers from him.

'I'm just busy,' I said. 'I'm going to see my grandfather today and I'm cooking for him. He loves my cooking so I have three things on the stove and two in the oven.'

'You've really embraced the concept of the domestic goddess,' he teased, yet it came out sounding more like a taunt.

'Eric, can I call you back?' His sarcasm turned me off. 'I don't want to burn anything.'

'Except me?'

Oh, God, I thought. 'What do you mean?' I asked innocently.

'I want to see you again, Ariana, but I get the feeling you're trying to blow me off.'

'I already did that, didn't I?' I just couldn't resist.

He was silent for a long moment. 'That's not why I want to see you again,' he said finally. 'I'd like to take you out to dinner so we can get to know each other better.'

The moment had come to tell him the truth, and uncomfortable as it made me what I felt for Gerald was infinitely stronger. 'Eric, I'm seeing someone else, and it's very serious.'

'I see.'

'I'm sorry…'

'I thought you came down to Miami for a funeral.'

'I did… that's where I met him.'

'So you already knew him when you fucked me?' He suddenly sounded hopeful.

'Yes, but… but I told you, that wasn't like me. I don't know what got into me…'

'I got into you, baby.'

His tone stoked a traitorous warmth in my pussy, yet it could never come close to burning away what I felt for Gerald, to whom my attraction was as intensely sensual as it was profound. 'I really loved fucking you, Eric,' I gave him that much, 'but I can't see you again. I'm sorry.'

'Don't be. Have a nice day with your grandfather. I'll call you again tomorrow to see if you've changed your mind. Believe it or not, I can be a very patient man.'

'Eric, please don't, I–' I never finished the sentence because the quality of the silence told me the connection had gone dead. He had fucked me twice wherever and however he pleased, and I sensed he was already addicted to the power I had given him. Yet I also knew it was a waste of time for me to try and understand why he had become so taken with me since all that mattered was protecting my budding relationship with Gerald. I was very glad Eric didn't know where I lived and that he was a police officer, because even though that meant he could obtain my address if he really wanted to, it also reassured me he wouldn't stalk me, which was something criminals did, not cops. I deliberately avoided the thought that for some reason he was temporarily suspended from duty. My intuition told me Eric was a good man and that I would most certainly have fallen into a relationship with him that could only have ended badly if I hadn't also met Gerald. My Magic Pattern had become erotically tangled, but it was a small price to pay for it having led me to my soul mate.

* * *

NOT JUST ANY ROAST CHICKEN

1 Whole Roasting Chicken, approximately 3-4 lbs
1 Lemon, sliced in half
Rosemary flavored Olive Oil
Minced Garlic
Sea Salt

Freshly Ground Black Pepper
Powdered Thyme
1 small Spanish Onion, peeled
Fresh Rosemary Sprigs
Dry White Wine (I use Chardonnay since I always have some on hand)
Organic Chicken Broth

Pre-heat the oven to 475° while you clean the Chicken, pat it dry with a paper towel and place it on a wire rack set in a glass oven pan. (It took me a long time to finally buy a wire rack, but I'm glad I did). Squeeze the fresh Lemon Juice over the chicken as well as into the cavity, reserving half the used lemon, then brush the bird with the Rosemary Olive Oil (I just use my fingertips) and season it inside and out (this is important) with the minced Garlic, Salt, freshly ground Black Pepper and the Thyme.

Stuff the peeled Onion into the cavity followed by the Lemon half and the fresh Rosemary sprigs, then fold the skin over the opening to seal them in. Pour a shallow pool of White Wine and Chicken Broth into the pan and bake at 475° for 15 minutes, then reduce the heat to 375° and bake another 60 minutes. At that point, remove the pan from the oven, pour in more Chardonnay if needed, and continue cooking the chicken until the internal temperature of a meat thermometer inserted between the leg and thigh reads 165° - 170° (about 30 minutes per pound.) When the chicken is done, thrust a fork into the cavity and let the juices flow out into the pan. I like to pour some of the juices over the chicken pieces and serve the rest in small bowls for dipping. Serve with white rice and a fresh green salad with cheese and you'll be in heaven.

NOT JUST LETTUCE SALAD

And to think I always threw away the Parsley sprig that often graced my plate in a restaurant thinking it was merely decoration, but the truth is Parsley is not only good for you, it also helps bring a salad to life.

Wash, dry and mix together equal portions of:
Chopped Romaine Lettuce
Chopped Curly Spinach
Chopped Fresh Parsley

Add:
Extra Sharp Cheddar Cheese, diced (to taste)
Salted Walnuts, chopped (to taste)
Tangerine Sections (optional & to taste)

Drizzle your favorite Light Olive Oil & Vinegar Dressing over the salad and toss well to mix. The less dressing you use, the better; this salad is already quite flavorful in itself. Better yet, just sprinkle it with Sea Salt and freshly ground Black Pepper, then drizzle equal amounts of Extra Virgin Olive Oil and Red Wine Vinegar over it.

MY GREEK SALAD

1 head Romaine Lettuce, washed and chopped

1 small Red Onion, thickly sliced and diced into approximately 1/2 inch pieces
2-3 large Tomatoes or 5-6 Plum Tomatoes, seeded and diced
Pitted Black Olives, chopped (to taste)
Crumbled Feta Cheese (be generous, Feta Cheese has less fat)
Sea Salt
Freshly Ground Black Pepper
Fresh Lemon Juice

I dislike the taste of most low-fat and fat-free salad dressings, so I improvised this "dressing-free" salad so rich in flavor you won't miss the oil and vinegar at all. Salt brings out the natural flavor of the lettuce, and the lemon juice mixes with the feta cheese to create a delicious creaminess offset by the spicy crunchiness of the red onion, which in turn is wonderfully mellowed by the black olives and balanced out by the plum tomatoes. This is a very satisfying salad that won't leave you hungering for "real" food afterwards.

HEALTHY CAESAR SALAD

1 1/2 Cups Soft Tofu
1/2 Cup Organic Low Sodium Chicken Broth
2 Garlic Cloves
4 tsp Dijon Mustard
Dash of Worcestershire Sauce
4-6 Anchovy Fillets (to taste)
1/2 tsp Sea Salt
1/4 tsp Freshly ground Black Pepper
1-2 Tbls Extra Virgin Olive Oil
1/4 Cup Soy Parmesan Cheese

Juice of 1 Lemon

Combine everything in a blender or a food processor (I personally use the easy-to-clean little container that came with my hand-held blender) and puree until smooth. This dressing tastes almost as decadent as the real thing and yet it's actually good for you. All you need now for a delicious Chicken Caesar Salad is 2 large Boneless-Skinless Chicken Breasts cut into bite-size chunks, and seasoned with Salt and Pepper then sautéed in a combination of Rosemary Olive Oil and Garlic Olive Oil. Serve the Chicken on a bed of chopped Romaine Lettuce and pour the Tofu Caesar dressing over them. This is one of my favorite quick and light, yet totally fulfilling, summer meals. This recipe makes enough to serve 2 people very generously or 4 people as a side dish.

CUBAN PICADILLO

1 pound Ground Sirloin
1-2 Tbls Extra Virgin Olive Oil
1 small Onion, chopped
2 tsp minced Garlic
1/4 cup Dry White Wine
1/2 can crushed Tomatoes
1 tsp Sea Salt
Freshly ground Black Pepper
1/3 cup pimiento-stuffed Green Olives, chopped

In a non-stick frying pan, cook the ground Sirloin over high heat until no longer pink, then transfer it to a plate with a slotted spoon, draining the fat out of the pan.

Add the Olive Oil to the hot pan. Reduce the heat to medium-low and sauté the Onion and Garlic, stirring often, for about five minutes.

Return the meat to the pan, turn the heat up to high again, and pour in the White Wine. Bring to a boil and cook for about one minute before adding the canned Tomatoes, the Sea Salt, and a very modest amount of freshly ground Black Pepper. Crush the Tomatoes a little with a wooden spoon, stir to mix, bring the mixture to a soft boil, and then reduce the heat to low.

Finally, add the pimento-stuffed Green Olives, cover the pan and simmer for thirty minutes or a little longer. Serve Picadillo with white rice and Plantains. (I prefer my Picadillo plain, but traditional garnishes are a hard-boiled egg finely chopped, 1/2 cup sweet peas and a chopped pimento.)

* * *

It was sweet spending time with my grandfather again, but after only about an hour I was figuratively climbing the walls of his studio apartment overlooking Coral Way. The constant sound of rushing traffic that would have driven me crazy seemed to help keep him company. Being elegantly frail and over ninety-years-old had done nothing to dampen his appetite; he devoured one-third of the chicken I had roasted for him while I enjoyed a big bowl of salad and mami settled for a modest portion of skin-free breast along with a small bowl of salad. That she was suddenly watching her weight further confirmed my suspicion that there was a serious man in the picture, but there was no chance of talking about him around abuelo; my grandfather would not approve, in fact, he was still trying to get over his daughter's divorce from my father years ago.

I painted a smile on my face and suffered through a host of family albums for what felt like the hundredth time. They contained faded black-and-white photographs of a time and place as romantic and as dead as the moon even though their physical setting was still only ninety miles away in Cuba. And while we were sitting on the couch with the past spread open across our laps, stooped and wrinkled specters of many of the people smiling with youthful radiance in the pictures dropped in to see me, for I was one of the family's principle roots in the present. I accepted countless dry wet kisses on my cheeks, and frail hugs from relatives I couldn't even remember the names of. They arrived in batches of two and three, literally holding each other up. Fortunately none of them stayed long or we would have run out of places for them to sit, but for most of the day the small space rang with lively energetic conversation defying the geriatric vocal chords producing it.

The sun was beginning to set when the flow of visitors ebbed, and it was a sad but sweet relief when mami and I finally said good bye to abuelo and drove home. My cell phone had been with me the whole time, of course, and at about three o'clock in the afternoon I was blessed with the wonderful intermission of a call from Gerald, which gave me the strength to deal with my family for the rest of the day. He would be picking me up later that evening on foot and taking me out to dinner. I couldn't wait.

* * *

Dressing to go out to dinner with a man always presents a bit of a conundrum for me – on the one hand I want to look as sexy as possible, on the other hand I don't want an overly tight outfit interfering with the pleasure I take in eating. I cannot imagine a more torturous scenario than a Victorian dinner table lined with pale women all wearing excruciatingly tight corsets that barely enabled them to make it through the soup coarse. We understand now why they were always fainting, undoubtedly from a lack of air, and probably also from nutritional deficit. In my opinion, real corsets belong in the bedroom and corset-style shirts – which have the sexy look of a corset but enable you to breathe – belong in the dining room. I myself own several such shirts, and I chose one of them for my date with Gerald that night. Maybe after my transgressions with Eric I needed to feel a little bit virginal, because I chose a white bridal-style corset-shirt that hooked closed in front just like the real thing and revealed only a modest amount of cleavage. The sleeves were my favorite part – transparent white veils that left most of my shoulders bare and clung lightly to my arms like a fine mist. I had just the right pair of silky black slacks to go with it, and black-strap sandals with thick high heels that would provide an elegant height as well as comfort for walking. I thought there was something very sexy about wearing pants with a corset-shirt; it struck me as a defiant blending of my feminine sexuality with my independent 'masculine' side. As I admired myself in the full length mirror, my outfit seemed to be saying, 'I have the power to do as I please, and it pleases me to be sexy and submissive to the right man's desires.' I didn't need a talking glass to tell me I looked fabulous. A small black purse just large enough to hold my cell phone, mirrored compact, lipstick, I.D., check-card and house key completed the ensemble.

Rosa was sitting in the living room watching the BBC World News when I emerged from my bedroom. 'Dios mio!' she exclaimed. 'Where did you get that… that shirt?'

'Some catalogue.' I sat down beside her on the couch.

'So where are you going for dinner?'

'I don't know. We're walking to Miracle Mile and there are dozens of places to choose from, as you know. We'll see what strikes our fancy.'

'Hmm,' she said, meaning 'If you don't pick one of the Italian restaurants, it's your culinary loss.'

On the television screen a bomb was going off on some nameless street in a part of the world I couldn't fathom living in. Then a woman dressed in black robes from head-to-toe was angrily holding up a photograph. Apparently, her husband had died in the blast. The volume was turned down so low I could barely hear her, but unfortunately I did. 'Now I'm one of those women who wants to be a suicide bomber!' she declared even while cradling a baby in one arm.

There was a quiet knock on the front door.

'That's him,' my mom said grimly, and I knew her tone related to the story on the news not to the man standing outside our house on the same planet yet in a totally different world.

I quickly rose to open the door, and when I saw Gerald standing on the threshold, I felt light-years removed from the pain and suffering the media constantly exposes us to. I was obeying completely different laws when I stepped towards him, and his arms came around me like the horizons of another dimension. That night he was wearing a black suit, and the way it contrasted with my white bodice for a magical instant elevated my senses to an arousing metaphysical point inside me free of all doubts and worries. His arms were a pure, dark force cradling me against his chest, and the sound of his heart beating was the pulse of time itself as I rested in the infinitely promising space of his arms.

CHAPTER TEN

I've discovered it's much easier to clearly remember an uncomfortable event than it is to recall the specifics of a totally happy one. Gerald and I walked hand-in-hand along the quiet residential streets of Coral Gables, then along the bustling luminous sidewalks branching out around Miracle Mile, talking and laughing; talking, and every now and then kissing without breaking our stride; talking and talking and talking. I began to realize just how curtailed my self-expression had been in previous relationships when I found myself telling Gerald what I thought and felt about things without needing to explain or justify my opinion. Not only did he understand exactly what I meant, he very often showed me the path of a perspective I had not realized was there before, leading me to a more fulfilling conclusion than I had believed possible. For example, when we were discussing politics and the environment, I stated a fact that felt like a dead-end there was no arguing with, and he lifted the leafy branch of my concept (made up of a life-time of accumulated thoughts) out of the way to show me I had not actually completed my thought; there was an opening out of my conclusion leading to a whole other side of things. Talking to Gerald proved such a rewarding experience that I kept opening up to him more and more, yet at the same time I seemed to know less and less about him. He had told me scarcely anything about his family, and every time I thought to ask him about them, another interesting topic came up in our conversation and I forgot.

We ended up in a little Italian restaurant (mami would be pleased) that was all light wood and brick and hanging plants. We were given a small private table in a corner next to the window looking out on the street. We sat facing each other, and only the arrival of the menus separated our hands, which were tightly clasped on the table. Gastronomia's specialty is home-made brick oven pizzas. The rest of their rather brief selection varies, but it is always flavorfully fresh. Being a relatively good cook who knows exactly what food costs, I always bristle a little when I first open a menu and look at the prices being charged for each dish, but that night I was too happy to care.

'We could always split a pizza,' Gerald suggested.

'Yes, but I don't really like pizza that much… I think I'd like to have the linguini with fresh clam sauce.'

'Mm, that does sound good,' he agreed, studying the menu, 'but I think I'll go for the spaghetti with shrimp and fresh basil. However, first I'm ordering us some Buffalo Mozzarella as an appetizer.'

'Great!'

'And now for the wine…'

I set down my menu and gazed in wonder at his handsome face

intently studying the wine list. 'I must have done something right,' I mused out loud.

He smiled at me. 'What was that?'

'I was just thinking that somebody Up There must like me.'

'Why?' he asked, but his smile deepened as though he knew.

'Because somehow I met you, Gerald.'

'Two deaths brought us together,' he reminded me quietly, closing his menu and resting it on top of mine.

'Life and death, two sides of the same coin... human existence is a truly mysterious currency. Do you really think it's worth anything in the end,' I looked hopefully into his eyes, 'or is buying into concepts of immortality a doomed investment; a counterfeit that just helps keep us happy?'

'Ariana,' he reached for my hand again, 'if you had asked me that a few days ago, I'm not sure what I would have said, but now,' he squeezed my hand fervently, 'I believe everything is possible.'

* * *

There's an intangible moment when good food and good wine and great company combine in a way that transcends time and space (or at least it feels that way) and past, present and future come together in a sense of infinite possibility. At some point during dinner that night, Gerald and I crossed over into that dimension where I finally learned some biographical facts about the man I already wanted to spend the rest of my life with. He was a Florida native, born and raised in Gainesville, which he had left years ago because he found the cultural and social scene too claustrophobic and limited. He said it was a beautiful place with lots of good qualities, but he had outgrown it. When he was ten-years-old, his grandmother bought him some modeling clay, and from that moment on he knew what he wanted to do when he grew up and forever after that. The path to sculpting for a living had not been easy, however, and he warned me it still wasn't and the odds were he would never be wealthy; in fact, he would be lucky if he could go on managing to make ends meet. When I hastened to assure him that money meant nothing to me, that I actually thrived on a budget, he smiled ruefully. 'Those filet mignons you made last night probably cost as much as my weekly food budget, Ariana.'

'It was a special occasion,' I pointed out. 'You can eat well without spending a lot of money, trust me, I've been doing it for years.'

'I do trust you, and the fact is I might make it one day.' He concentrated on his food for a moment. 'My friend, the one who owns the gallery you saw my piece in, he called me today… he sold it.'

'That's fabulous!' I exclaimed, then was abruptly hit by an entirely different sentiment. 'But how could you bear to part with it? It's so beautiful!'

'Don't worry, I can always recast it. I made quite a lot of money off it.'

'You deserve it. It's the most beautiful piece of work I've seen in a long time.'

'Now you're lying, Ariana.'

'I am not lying, it's–'

'You looked in the mirror this evening when you were getting dressed, didn't you?'

I laughed.

'I have to confess, Ariana… I've started a new piece, inspired by you. I hope you won't be offended, but I never put clothes on my statues, rarely, anyway.'

'Why on earth would I be offended? I'm honored.'

So our conversation progressed, during which he confessed to occasionally working as a massage therapist to make ends meet. 'I got a degree in Massage Therapy thinking, what the hell, it's a lot like sculpting except I'm kneading living flesh, and it's oddly relaxing for me because there's no pressure to mold and shape it to my will. I'm not trying to bring it to life, I'm just kneading and caressing, kneading and squeezing. I think of it as a good sculptor's work-out.'

'You're a massage therapist?' I asked in awe. 'I'd have a full body massage every week if I could afford it.'

'Well, now you can.'

'Oh, I didn't mean I want you to feel obliged to give me—'

'Ariana.'

He said my name so firmly I almost gasped, 'Yes, Gerald?' because how serious he suddenly looked worried me.

'I never feel obliged to do anything, Ariana. Whatever I do, it's because I want to do it, so if you find yourself getting full body massages every week from now on, then relax secure in the knowledge that I'm doing it because I want to do it; because it pleases me as much, perhaps even more, as it pleases you.'

'Yes, Gerald, thank you, that means a lot to me. I… I've been with so many men who did things because they felt they had to or because it was what everyone else was doing or because it was a means-to-an end for them, not a pleasure in itself… do you know what I mean?'

'There are a lot of lost people out there, Ariana, but they need not concern us anymore. We have each other now.'

Finally, I was rendered speechless with happiness.

* * *

Parting from him that night was one of the hardest things I've ever done in my life. The only thing that made it possible for me was the knowledge he would be coming for me again first thing in the morning. I would be spending the whole day with him tomorrow at his studio, which was also his apartment. Nevertheless, saying good bye or anything else was still nearly impossible because we couldn't stop kissing. No words were needed then to express how I felt about him; body language took over and felt much more eloquent than any of the conversations we'd had all evening. The sensations of my arms wrapped around his neck and our tongues wrestling and his buried erection digging into my belly as his hands squeezed my ass all added up to one indelible fact – I wanted him to possess me, to take me, to make love to me, to fuck me... there was no completely satisfying way to express the hot, urgent reality of my need. He had walked me home, but then it took us a small eternity to make it to the front door as the arms of a centuries-old tree welcomed us beneath it and it wasn't at all easy to escape its dark, deep hospitality. At one point I separated myself from him in order to caress his broad shoulders in awe of their strength and firmness, such an arousing contrast to his lean hips and long legs.

'It's no wonder you're a sculptor when you're built like a classical statue yourself,' I told him, reaching up to caress the freshly-shaved smoothness of his face with both hands. His cheeks were just the slightest bit plump, like a boy's, a totally endearing compliment to his firm mouth and elegant nose. 'You have the most beautiful body, Gerald.' I slipped my hands into his suit jacket, and felt my way down to his belt, then impatiently past it, cupping his hard-on in my right palm while my other hand reached behind him and grasped one of his tight ass cheeks. 'Mm, I don't think I can wait anymore...' I snapped open his belt and fumbled with the button holding his pants closed.

'Ariana, are you sure–'

'Yes, please,' I begged. 'You didn't buy me desert, it's the least you could do.' I wrested the button free and yanked down his zipper. He helped me then, and I thought maybe he had been expecting this or at least hoping for it because he was wearing black underwear with a convenient flap opening in the front through which he pulled his cock out for me with one hand and lifted his balls out with the other, his male organs shoved enticingly up and out by the tight elastic. I promptly sank to my knees. It was so dark beneath the canopy of leaves I wouldn't have been able to see anything if not for the diffused golden glow of a streetlight enabling me to make out his erection's glorious dimensions. I couldn't help thinking that for some reason his penis was much more beautiful and more sensitive-looking than Eric's, perhaps because of the way the head distinguished itself from the shaft, giving it more of a mysterious personality, and because its impressive length wasn't a straight boring rod either, thickening somewhat towards the middle in a way I knew would feel wonderful inside me. I felt perfectly happy kneeling in the grass in the dark at his feet as I allowed his cock to slide slowly between my lips, and it thrilled me to experience his mental surprise and physical joy when I took his full length into my mouth and let his head nuzzle my throat.

'Oh, Ariana!' he breathed, gently taking hold of my skull as though he was afraid of going to far, and yet also giving himself the power to do so if he couldn't resist.

I relished the taste and feel of him for a moment before letting him glide all the way off my tongue so I could look up at him and speak. 'I want you to fuck my mouth,' I heard myself say fervently. 'Please, Gerald, fuck my mouth!'

'Ariana, I–'

'Oh, God, just fuck my mouth, please, I mean it, just fuck it, I want you to, I want you to fuck my mouth! Please fuck my mouth, please fuck my mouth,' I whispered like a mantra.

He didn't say anything; he merely took firm hold of my hair with both hands and did as I asked. He thrust his erection between my lips again and pushed my head back so he could ram himself all the way down into my neck. I thought I would die from the pleasure as he fucked my mouth just like I wanted him to, stimulating his head with my throat and caressing the full length of his shaft with my tongue and lips by pulling almost all the way out of me after every one of his fast, hard strokes. I had to cling to his slacks to brace myself, but with his every penetration I felt better and better, as if his semen was cleansing my soul's palate of the mysteriously bad aftertaste of another man's pleasure and making me his completely. The arduous exercise made my heart race with joy because the longer it went on the more I belonged to him and the more deeply I knew he felt for me. I was sacrificing comfort and breath for his ultimate pleasure and it brought us together in the hauntingly absolute way I longed for with him. When he climaxed it was so deep in my mouth I barely felt or tasted his cum spurting down my throat, but the helpless pulsing of his hard-on resting on my tongue and trapped between my lips was exquisite and filled me with a profound satisfaction that defied all logic.

He had come with just a sexy catch of his breath, and he remained silent as he reached down and helped me to my feet, understanding that my knees were a little stiff from kneeling and a little weak from the intense pleasure I had taken in serving him. I watched regretfully as he somehow got his still impressive erection back in his underpants, and the sound of his zipper going up was a strangely exciting, electric note to me in the sexual symphony of crickets and cicadas calling to potential mates in the darkness.

'Oh, Ariana…' He took me in his arms and crushed me almost painfully against him, once again taking my breath away. Then he walked me up to the front door of the house, and after one last lingering kiss said, 'Good night, dear, I'll see you in the morning.'

'Good night,' I echoed. Worn out from serving him, I found the strength to let go of him for a few hours.

* * *

When I entered the house, I saw the back of mami's blonde head watching television just as I left her with the only difference being there was now a man's dark-haired head beside hers. I paused on the threshold not quite able to register the sight of my mom's blonde hair resting on a man's shoulder; my emotional software performed an immediate emergency upgrade as I stood there taking in the innocent yet distressingly significant scene. I suffered a stab of irrational jealousy at having to share my mother's love and affection with someone else, but fortunately my totally fulfilling evening with Gerald clipped the rush of selfish emotion right in the bud. Nevertheless, it felt very strange to step inside from the dark jungle-like yard where I had just sucked a man down – where I had just had my mouth and throat fucked as hard as a cunt, to be more precise – and suddenly land in the midst of content domesticity; a serene atmosphere completely different from the sexual tempest I had just experienced outside. The couple on the couch hadn't heard the key turn in the lock or the door open and close, but the man's hearing seemed instinctively honed to the sound of high-heels crossing ceramic tiles because he turned his head, and smiled happily when he saw me.

'Hola, Ariana, did you have a nice time?'

'Ernesto!' I cried.

My mother smiled dreamily back at me. 'Why are you so surprised?' she asked mildly.

'Because… because you've been friends for years!'

'Can you think of a better foundation for a relationship?' Ernesto asked reasonably.

Rosa's tone sharpened, 'So where did you finally decide to eat?'

'Gastronomia,' I replied with relief.

She beamed at me. 'Oh, that's a nice place, although Café–'

'Well, good night!' I declared before she could launch into a full-length description of her favorite Italian restaurants and the best dishes to be found at each one. 'Um, I'm glad... I'm glad it's you, Ernesto,' I added awkwardly.

His grin softened into a gentle smile that made me feel like a little girl at heart even with my hair wantonly disheveled and my face flushed from the arduous blow-job I had just given another man. 'I'm glad, too, Ari. Sweet dreams. By the way, that's quite a nice... shirt.'

'Good night, Ari,' my mother echoed peacefully, her head coming to rest on the strong shoulder beside hers again. 'It's a corset shirt,' she explained. 'She ordered it from a catalogue.'

'Mm, I like it. Maybe we should order you one...'

'Good night!' I repeated loudly, and escaped to my side of the house.

My bedroom was dark. I switched on two lamps, and tossed my purse carelessly onto the dresser even though it contained my precious cell phone. I wouldn't need its technological crutch for a while, thank God; Gerald was walking over in the morning and taking me to breakfast, then we would be heading for his place where I would have the pleasure of watching him work for a while. I was also curious to see the new piece he had begun inspired by me. I was so fulfilled by the evening, and so much looking forward to the following day that I felt at once languid and impatient, as though I was suspended outside of time and I wanted it desperately to keep flowing; I wished it was morning already. I began undoing my shirt (which required almost as much work as a real corset) while unconsciously pacing the room, vaguely aware of the smile on my lips as I re-lived those arduous yet intensely satisfying moments beneath a tree. I was in no rush to brush my teeth. It pleased me the last thing in my mouth had been Gerald's cock and that its subtly wonderful flavor still lingered on my tongue. For some unfathomable reason, he had tasted better to me than any other man ever had.

My Barbie dolls all looked particularly happy tonight, even the one I had flung carelessly down earlier when Eric called. Remembering that, I thought about how incredibly slutty my behavior had been since I landed in Miami, but my profound happiness immediately shrugged off any potentially guilty perspective on recent events. Looked at another way, I had been unbelievably lucky since I arrived in Miami, and I felt more beautifully alive and hopeful than I ever had in my life. I lovingly positioned the recumbent doll back on her place at the table sitting on top of a pile of leather-bound books crowned by Grim's Fairytales. I crossed her long plastic legs, leaned her back on her cold arms, and left her smiling cheerfully up at the blank ceiling in her sexy red halter-top, black mini-skirt and boots as I slipped out of my own clothes, the living warmth of my flesh hauntingly accentuated for me by the presence of my dolls. I carelessly kicked off my heels, but draped my slacks and shirt carefully over a chair for they had been part of my wonderful night with Gerald and as a result I would always fondly remember this particular outfit. My life suddenly felt better than any game I had ever played, and for a moment, as I prepared to slip off my panties, I held my breath possessed by the arousing sense of being poised on a threshold between fantasies and reality – Gerald's presence on earth proved there truly could be an open door between them. I felt we were stepping through into this other fourth dimension together; a dimension that had always been there existing alongside the normal three dimensions, but it had been mysteriously inaccessible until our souls met and merged and mysteriously opened the door to it.

I slipped on a red silk robe since there was a man in the house, and went to perform my ritual ablutions in the bathroom, where my thoughts became more practical but no less elated as a result. I thanked God that as a freelance columnist for online (as well as a handful of print) magazines I could live anywhere. I was still faced with the daunting task of moving all my possessions down from Boston to Miami, yet I knew I could handle it. I felt I could handle anything now that I had met Gerald. As long as I can handle his beautiful cock every day, I thought, and was overwhelmed with excitement for a few moments trying to imagine what he would feel like inside me.

Back in my bedroom, I shrugged off the robe, grabbed one of my notebooks, and propped happily up in bed. I was too keyed up to go to sleep just yet, and more and more I was possessed by the serious desire to try and publish a cookbook. At the very least, I wanted to organize all my own personal favorite recipes, so I stayed up writing out some of my latest culinary creations, until I at last felt sleepy enough to set my notebook aside, turn off the light and go to sleep dreaming about tomorrow.

PAN-GRILLED RAINBOW TROUT

2 Medium-sized Whole Rainbow Trout, cleaned and gutted, head and tail removed
Extra Virgin Olive Oil
Sea Salt
Freshly Ground Black Pepper
2 tsp Minced Garlic
Powdered Thyme

Fresh or dried Rosemary Sprigs
1 Whole Lemon sliced in half

I once shied away from cooking whole fish myself until I began doing some of my shopping in large oriental markets where you can have any fish you desire cleaned and gutted for you, and the head and tail removed as well. I don't know exactly why, but a whole fish is more flavorful than a fillet and, as it turns out, just as easy to prepare. All you have to do when you bring your cleaned Trout home are rinse them and season them to taste with the above ingredients.

Begin by brushing the Trout with the Olive Oil, season them with the Sea Salt and the Pepper (both inside and out) dust the cleaned cavities with the powdered Thyme, then add the Garlic to the cavity, using about 1 tsp for each fish. Finally, gently stuff them with some Rosemary sprigs and cook on a pre-heated electric grill (or in a grill pan) for approximately five minutes on each side. You'll be able to tell when the fish are cooked by the way the meat flakes when you test it with a fork, and it will also be opaque now instead of translucent. Remove the Rosemary sprigs from the cavity before serving each Trout with a lemon half, and with small plates on which to discard the skin and bones.

All you need now is a big salad of Romaine Lettuce and Spinach with Tomatoes and chunks of extra sharp Cheddar Cheese very lightly drizzled with your favorite light Vinaigrette (it may be fashionable at the moment, but Balsamic Vinegar has such a strong flavor it can overwhelm a salad's delicate ingredients, so I prefer to use a traditional Red Wine Vinegar & Olive Oil dressing). Add an easily opened can of Creamed Corn and you'll have a totally satisfying low-fat dinner for two.

CUBAN RED SNAPPER

2 Small-to-Medium-Sized Whole Red Snappers, cleaned and gutted
Extra Virgin Olive Oil
Juice of 1 Lime
Sea Salt
Freshly Ground Black Pepper
Minced Garlic

Brush the fish with a generous amount of Extra Virgin Olive Oil and then squeeze the Lime juice over it. Season it inside and out with the Sea Salt and freshly ground Black Pepper, then with your fingertips spread about 1 tsp of Garlic into each cavity. Now all you need to do is grill them for about five minutes on each side, and serve. These babies are just too delicious for words.

OVEN-FRIED GROUPER FILLETS

2 Grouper Fillets (about 1 pound total)
Sea Salt
Freshly Ground Black Pepper
1 Egg
2 Tbls Lemon Juice
1/3 Cup Flour
1 Cup Unseasoned Bread Crumbs
2 Tbls Butter

This is your classic oven-fried breading recipe, and Grouper is such a flavorful fish it really works, although you can use any other fish you desire, of course. Lightly season the fillets with the Sea Salt and the freshly ground Black Pepper as you preheat the oven to 350°, then in a shallow bowl beat the Egg with the Lemon juice.

Smooth the Flour across a small plate, and the Bread Crumbs across a second larger plate.

Coat the Fish Fillets with the Flour, dip them into the Egg-and-Lemon mixture, then coat them with the Bread Crumbs. (If you have left over flour, egg and bread crumbs, repeat the procedure for an even thicker, more satisfying crust.)

In a shallow baking dish (never use non-stick if you can avoid it) melt the Butter and place the Fillets on top. Bake for 20-30 minutes, testing for doneness after 20 minutes.

CHAPTER ELEVEN

Gerald was right on time. The antique clock in the hall had just struck nine times when the doorbell rang – a beautiful sympho-ny to my ears. I was ready to go, and starving. Gastronomia's clam sauce had been good, but there hadn't been enough of it to sat-isfy me, and I had seriously exerted myself afterwards.

Today I had chosen to wear a relatively short black cotton skirt that fell loosely over my bare thighs, and a short-sleeved navy-blue V-neck cotton T-shirt that looked very cute beneath the pony-tail I had gathered my hair up into. And since Gerald had warned me his studio resembled a bomb site, I was wearing black sneakers and socks. If I had had any doubts about my appearance, the expression in his eyes as I opened the door and he looked me up and down would immediately have dispersed them. Mami was still in bed, alone; Ernesto's car was no longer parked behind hers. I had been so completely wrapped up in Gerald last night I hadn't even noticed the driveway on the other side of the house, much less the extra car in it. Ernesto would be back that afternoon, however. He was picking mami up and they were spending a couple of days down in Key West, which meant I would have the house all to myself.

I fervently hugged and kissed Gerald in the foyer, but we didn't linger. 'I really need some coffee,' he confessed, 'so if you don't mind...'

'Not at all, I'm ready to go.' I snatched up my purse.

He smiled. 'Only how beautiful you look is keeping me awake. I'm afraid I'm not a morning person.'

'I would love some coffee myself, and some food. Let's go.'

He eyed me suspiciously as I locked the front door behind us. 'You're much too full of energy for someone who hasn't had any caffeine yet.'

'Oh, yes, I'm a morning person, I'm afraid. It's when I do my best writing, when my brain is still fresh.'

He groaned as he took my hand, and squeezed it as if by way of a fond reprimand. 'My brain doesn't kick into gear until afternoon.'

I laughed, surreptitiously looking him up and down as we walked. He was wearing a short-sleeved black t-shirt over old blue jeans, black sneakers and dark sunglasses he had slipped up onto his head when we were inside, but which he immediately pulled down over his eyes as we began walking. He looked good enough to eat, literally. 'That's a good idea,' I said, fishing my sunglasses out of my purse.

'Hmm, I like those,' he admitted, 'which is strange because normally I despise leopard print on anything.'

'So do I, believe me, but for some reason these appealed to me.'

'They look great on you, but then you could make anything look good.' He squeezed my hand again affectionately, possessively, and the gesture made me inexpressibly happy.

It was a beautiful day in south Florida. The sky was a radiant blue strikingly enhanced by the tinted lenses over my eyes, and the deep green of Coral Gable's splendid old trees rising everywhere around us was outlined against the earth's atmosphere with such stunning clarity every individual leaf seemed significantly visible that morning. Even the temperature was cooler than normal for the time of year, even though I knew that in an hour or two it would once again be hellishly hot beneath the sun. Yet in those moments as we walked in the direction of Miracle Mile intent on getting some breakfast, everything looked, and felt, perfect.

'I'm warning you, Ariana, my apartment isn't exactly what you would call cozy.'

Now it was my turn to squeeze his hand reassuringly. 'I know, Gerald, you told me. It's your studio.'

'Yes.'

'What's wrong?' I asked, because his mouth had hardened almost imperceptibly but in a way I was already sensitive to; the slightest sign of his displeasure upset and worried me.

'I'm just thinking,' he replied ambiguously.

'Thinking about what?' I queried anxiously.

'I'm thinking about the fact that you live up in Boston, and that where I live is barely big enough for me and my statuesque roommates.'

'Oh... I told you in the funeral home that I was thinking of moving back down to Miami, Gerald, and now... well, now I'm not just thinking about it. I mean, I really want to move back down now.' I held my breath.

'Good,' he said firmly. 'I'm licensed to drive a truck, you know. I can fly up to Boston with you and help you move your stuff down.'

'Really?'

He flashed me a luminous smile beneath the dark panes of his sunglasses. 'Really.'

'That would be wonderful, but you don't need to, I could just hire professional–'

'Ariana, what did I tell you last night?'

'You told me a lot of things, Gerald,' I pointed out, buying myself some time to figure out what he was referring to specifically.

'Yes, but you know what I'm talking about.'

To my surprise, I realized I did. 'You said you never did anything unless you really wanted to.'

'Very good. Try and remember that.'

'I will,' I promised, 'it's just that I've never met anyone like you before.'

'I've been married once,' he confessed out of the blue. 'It was a long time ago and I was very young. It ended quickly and badly.'

I almost said, 'I'm sorry' but stopped myself from uttering such an obvious hypocrisy; I wasn't at all sorry he was divorced. I was very glad his marriage had turned out badly even if I was sorry he had had to suffer as a result.

'I've been a bachelor for years,' he added.

I remained silent, encouraging his confidential mood.

'And I haven't exactly been celibate, if you know what I mean.'

'I can imagine!' I said with feeling. A man as good looking as he was could be sleeping with half-a-dozen women at a time if he really wanted to. Not to mention the fact that he was a sculptor and they were notorious for seducing their beautiful naked models... I felt the green serpent of jealousy painfully uncoiling in my belly, and tried desperately to stamp it down before it got its fangs of fear and insecurity into my heart. 'I haven't been exactly virginal myself,' I confessed shortly.

'Virgins are highly overrated.'

I glanced at him, and when I saw he was smiling softly at me, everything was all right with the world again. I was glad he had told me what he had; it made me feel less guilty about Eric, who would get my voicemail if he tried calling me today because I had deliberately left my cell phone at home.

We had breakfast in a small Cuban café sitting at the counter. The orange juice was deliciously fresh, squeezed right there in front of us, and well worth the wait. The café con leches were wonderful, just the right blend of coffee and foaming white milk; Cuban toast is always good; and my two eggs-over-easy were prepared perfectly and not too greasy. Gerald ordered a second coffee and we lingered contentedly over the counter for a while even after we finished eating. We had missed the pre-work breakfast rush, but the place was obviously popular, and it was fun people watching for a while as we talked about everything and nothing. Then at last it was time to head for his studio. I braced myself for the daunting mess he had lead me to expect there even as I could scarcely wait to see more examples of his work, especially the new piece he had begun, the one inspired by me.

'I should tell you a little about the materials I use,' he said when we were on our way again. He lived on the same side of 42nd Avenue my mother did, and we were soon back on the quiet residential streets west of Miracle Mile. 'I like to use moist, water-based clay with no grog in it.'

I laughed. 'Grog?'

'It's used by potters. It's a finely ground fired clay added to the clay body to give it extra strength and a gritty texture.'

'Oh.'

'Sometimes I also use oil-based clay, but my technique tends to involve a lot of water and brush work and lots of clay, so mostly I use water-based clay.'

'How do you keep it moist while you're working?' I asked curiously. 'I've played around with small amounts of water-based clay and it always dries out on me really fast.'

'Well, as you know, modeling clay comes wrapped in plastic, moist and ready to work, and once you open the wrapping it begins drying out, so what you need to do is keep it wrapped in a plastic trash-can liner inside a plastic trash can with a lid. It's also a good idea to lay a wet towel on top of it before closing the plastic. As for whatever piece I'm working on at the moment, I keep it wrapped in a damp cloth with plastic over it.'

'And when you're done with it, do you fire it in a kiln like potters do?'

'That all depends. If what I want is to make a plaster mold from my finished sculpture, I can't let it dry out. Once it's dry I'd have to make a rubber mold from it. If what I want is to have my finished sculpture cast, then I don't need to worry about the kind of armature I use or how I apply the clay since the mold only picks up the surface of the sculpture. What's inside or how it's constructed doesn't matter.'

'Um, okay.' He was losing me, but it was interesting listening to him nonetheless.

He laughed. 'You'll understand it all better once you see it.'

'If you say so. Do you just use your hands to shape the sculpture?'

'I love to use my hands.' He let go of mine for an instant to caress and squeeze my ass. 'But I can't always just use my hands. I probably have as many modeling tools as you do kitchen utensils. There's a shape for every conceivable need. I have lots of wire-end tools, all kinds of brushes, from fine watercolor brushes to a common household whisk. I often use wet and dry brushes to blend and model and smooth the surface of the clay. Then there's all the miscellaneous stuff I need – wire screens, burlap cloths, cheese cloths, old rags of all shapes and sizes, textured materials, pieces of flexible cardboard, etc. etc.'

'What on earth do you use all those things for?'

'I use them to blend the clay and to model and texture the surface, of course. And I love Tupperware.'

I laughed again. 'Tupperware?'

'Oh, yes, I'm a big Tupperware fan. It's great for storing wet clay, dry clay, water, and all my tools, although I often use clay flower pots for tool holders; they're more aesthetic. Then I have sheers and wire snips for cutting wire screening, and of course several plastic plant misters to wet down my sculpture while I'm working on it.'

His studio was located in a quaint old building containing only four apartments. The stone exterior was a faded buttercup yellow, and I saw right away how the living spaces inside would appeal to an artist because every residence appeared to possess three lovely bay windows.

'A friend of mine owns the building,' he told me as we made our way up the central staircase inside. 'That's how I can afford to live here. He doesn't need to worry about renovating the apartment so he lets me have it for cheap. He also professes to be an art lover, although what I really think is that he's gay and half in love with me not with my clay nudes.' He slipped of his sunglasses to wink at me as with his other hand he deftly thrust a key into the lock and opened the door.

I stepped past him into a surprisingly spacious interior flooded with sunlight. 'Oh, my God,' I said beneath my breath, quickly removing my shades to better see all the naked bodies crowding the room. They weren't sculptures in the Classical sense, virtuous nudes standing with their hands modestly covering their sex. The men and women in Gerald's studio were all overtly sensual, and many of them were engaged in some erotic act or another just like the polished black piece of the man and woman making love I had scene in the gallery. 'Oh, my God,' I repeated.

'I told you it was a mess,' he apologized.

'That's not what I meant!' I quickly put my purse down on one of the windowsills and reverently approached one of the clay couples. Their arms and legs were wrapped around each other in such a way that it was almost impossible to tell where the man ended and the woman began, but their bodies were clearly masculine and feminine even though their heads were half merged in an impossibly deep kiss. The piece was life-sized and almost perfectly egg-shaped where it sat on a waist-high pedestal, and it was the same highly polished black material of the piece I had seen in the gallery. It was at once intensely erotic and starkly metaphysical and I absolutely loved it.

Tempted as I am, I'll refrain from launching into a description of all of Gerald's pieces, suffice to say that as I walked around them in admiring wonder, I felt as though I was in an enchanted forest full of mythical lovers either caught in moments of passionate union or lying alone evocatively touching themselves whilst reaching out to their invisible heart's desire. Their creator had moved humbly over to a luminous corner of the room while I studied his work, silently letting me take it in, and it was a while before I turned to him and said, 'These are unbelievable.'

'I'm glad you like them,' he said matter-of-factly.

'Like them?! They're…they're amazing!' I declared almost angrily, because I couldn't seem to find the words to describe how his work made me feel. Then I saw he had slipped on a full-length white apron like the kind worn by chefs and was caressing a prone woman's smooth brown buttocks. I approached him curiously even as I fell respectfully silent, because he had begun working and I sensed he was already only half aware of me… or at least he was only half aware of my living presence; most of his attention was now focused on my clay body. Even though all I could see was her backside, I somehow knew it was my spread thighs he was squeezing and stroking. I watched him in reverent fascination, half hypnotized and half seduced by his hands' constant back-and-forth movements mostly concentrated on my hips and waist. He seemed to repeat the same procedures more than once, blurring and redefining my clay flesh in a process I gradually realized consisted of building up and carving away, smoothing over and roughening the surface until each individual element of my developing figure became part of a harmonious whole.

'You know, Ariana,' he spoke abruptly without looking back at me, 'your mouth is the exact same shape I've always given the mouth of my female sculptures. Did you notice?'

I looked around me again at all the female faces actually visible in the hauntingly silent forest of sexually charged bodies. I had thought it was only my imagination it was my face smiling back at me everywhere. 'Yes, I see…'

'For the mouth I use two coils of clay,' he informed me in an academic tone as he continued working, 'one for the upper lip and one for the lower lip, and I press them into position. Basically, the features are added to the original head shape, the chin, the ears, and so on.'

I walked slowly around my recumbent clay form. One of my cheeks was resting on my arms bent comfortably beneath my head. 'I don't have a face.' I was somewhat shocked by the featureless egg not yet cracked by any personality whatsoever.

'Not yet. I'm working my way up.'

'I see,' I repeated, this time walking behind him as I circled the piece. Just looking at him made me want to touch him, but I refrained from distracting him, and instead peered curiously at my water-based sex. 'Is that why you studied my pussy so intently the other night?' I asked, rather pleased with the shape of my labia, and intrigued by the dark opening glistening provocatively at the heart of my clay vulva.

'That's one of the reasons, although I don't need a reason to look at your pussy other than the sheer pleasure it gives me.' When he suddenly thrust the ball of his thumb between my sex lips and lovingly smoothed their edges I felt the gesture between my living legs. I realized then my panties were uncomfortably damp. And as if my physiological responses were mysteriously linked to the earth's atmosphere the studio darkened abruptly as the sun disappeared behind a cloud. My pulse quickened as a wave of darkness flowed over the statues and they seemed to absorb it naturally, almost hungrily...

'A storm is brewing,' I announced quietly.

He didn't answer as he stepped over to a sink in the corner and began washing his hands.

I continued studying my clay self lying across a bare wooden table. 'It looks as though I'm sleeping,' I observed.

'You are,' he confirmed, removing his apron and hanging it from a bare nail thrusting out of the wall, 'and you're dreaming of me fucking you.'

Far away outside the sky groaned ominously, yet I was so turned on the sound seemed full of haunting promise.

'And fuck you is what I'm going to do right now, Ariana. Take off your clothes.'

Surrounded as I was by naked bodies, all of whom had been shaped by his skilled hands, I didn't hesitate to obey. I pulled off my shirt first, pleased by the pale perfection of my breasts, beautifully firm and round when I'm aroused and a strangely thrilling contrast to all the hard black bosoms in the room.

'Keep going,' he urged quietly, removing his own shirt.

The sight of his naked chest sparsely covered with black hairs momentarily distracted me from the task of pushing down my shorts and panties, but I quickly stepped out of them as he began unbuttoning his jeans. Now the moment had come, I felt I couldn't wait another second to feel his cock inside me.

'Tale your sneakers off, too,' he instructed. 'I want you completely naked.'

I did as he said even though the wooden floor at my feet was littered with some rather dangerous-looking instruments. I could tell my work would be cut out for me domestically (personally, I thrive on neatness and cleanliness) but I didn't care. I already knew I would do whatever I had to do to spend the rest of my life with this man, who I felt to be magnificent in every sense, not just physically. Now my discarded clothing contributed to the general chaos of the place even as I felt everything coming together inside me beneath his admiring gaze.

'I think your ponytail is adorable, but I want you to let your hair down. I don't want anything constricting you.'

I pulled the navy-blue elastic off, dropped it on top of my shirt, and shook my hair loose around my shoulders.

'You're beautiful, Ariana, do you know that?'

'I feel beautiful with you, Gerald.'

'That's good, because you're mine.' He kicked off his own sneakers and stood completely naked before me. Lightning flashed outside and defined all his firm muscles for me in a flash of silver light reflecting my profound excitement as distant thunder rumbled like an echo of the blood rushing through my heart as he moved towards me.

'Come here,' he said gently, and taking my hand, he led me over to one of the windows. 'It's all right,' he assured me when I hesitated instinctively. 'No one ever looks up. Their loss.'

I looked down at the deserted street, then up at the sky almost as black now as the sculptures behind us. Sudden thunderstorms are common in Miami during the summer months; you can almost set your watch by them. This particular atmospheric disturbance was early, however (they usually occur later in the day) and judging by the color of the heavens promised to be a powerful one. There wasn't a soul in sight, and even the birds had taken cover from the impending deluge. There was no one to see the two naked bodies standing in the window or to watch as they turned towards each other, the man taking the woman roughly in his arms and bending her back as he kissed her passionately.

I would have let him fuck me right there in plain sight of anyone who happened to walk or drive by, yet I admit to being relieved when he took my hand again and led me to the other side of the studio. His small bedroom was dark, and almost completely filled by a king-size waterbed neatly covered by a black comforter and messily crowned by at least half-a-dozen pillows of assorted colors. Until that day I considered waterbeds undesirable relics from the seventies, but I have since revised my opinion. The firm softness deliciously engulfed us as we lay down side-by-side, and stared into each other's shadowed eyes for a long moment before he abruptly rolled on top of me. It crossed my mind the 'missionary position' wasn't very exciting, but I understood and shared his urgency. The important thing was to get him inside me; to feel his erection opening my pussy up around it for the first time. More radical positions would come soon enough. He supported his weight on both arms as I reached down between our bodies to grasp his hard-on hungrily in my hand.

'Oh, yes,' I whispered, 'let me put it inside me slowly... oh, yes...' I relished the sensation of his swollen head pushing between the slick folds of my labia, then the experience of his full length slowly filling me. His cock was thick and long and just the right mysterious dimensions to fill my pussy so completely my soul felt as though it had finally come home. I reached behind him and squeezed his ass with both hands as I pushed him all the way down inside me. 'Oh, Gerald!' I gasped.

'Put your hands above your head,' he commanded.

It was my great pleasure to obey him.

'I'm going to fuck you,' he warned quietly. 'I have to fuck you, Ariana.'

'Oh, yes, please, fuck me,' I begged shamelessly. 'Fuck me as hard as you want to, please...'

He groaned as he pulled almost all the way out of me before ramming himself back into my pussy with such force it literally took my breath away. I spread my legs as wide as possible, longing to give him full access to my wet, clinging depths, and for some reason only feeling us joined at the sex intensified my fulfillment almost unbearably. His muscular arms rose around me like snake-entwined columns as he fucked me with an intense relentless energy that had me clutching one of the soft pillows behind me as my flesh gladly absorbed his violent thrusts. I was barely aware of my cries as the sound of the deluge outside seemed to fill the waterbed itself, and his swift penetrations seemed to be happening in rhythm with the lightning flashing outside as well as in all my nerve-endings. He banged me remorselessly, pulling almost all the way out of me with every stroke so he could shove the full, rending length of his hard-on into my tight cunt over and over again.

'Oh, yes,' I moaned. 'Fuck me, fuck me hard...' I really hadn't believed he could drive into me with more force and was thrilled to discover I was wrong when his hips pummeled mine mercilessly as his rampant penis stabbed me so fiercely and deeply I almost couldn't stand the ecstasy. I knew when he started coming because how thick and hard his cock got, straining my sex wide open around the pulsing shaft, began pushing my clitoris over the edge into a climax...

'Oh, Ariana...' He collapsed into my arms as he ejaculated, and very nearly took me with him as he kept pounding into my pussy and delighting me with his efforts to prolong the joy of our bodies coming together for the first time.

We lay in each other's arms afterwards listening to the sound of the rain on the leaves outside the window and to our own quiet breathing, and I for one rested content with my head on his chest, silently thanking the Powers That Be for the deep, thunder-like beat of this man's heart beneath me.

* * *

When we finally rose from his heavenly waterbed, Gerald very reluctantly showed me his kitchen. I refrained from wincing in pain at how small it was, and there were indeed books in the oven on both shelves. There was no toilet paper in the refrigerator (he confessed to having removed it earlier knowing I would be coming over) but there wasn't much else in it either, just a few suspiciously old looking bottles of condiments and a slimy stick of butter I promptly threw in the garbage. The contents of the freezer shocked and appalled me; it was stuffed full of Healthy Choice frozen dinners. I had wondered how this man survived with just old mustard and ketchup in his refrigerator, now I knew, and the knowledge depressed me. There were boxes of pasta in the cupboards (naturally) an assortment of exotic condiments such as Mango Chutney, countless jars of Hot Salsa, an odd assortment of pans and utensils, and enough mismatched stainless steel forks to equip a cheap Diner.

'Why on earth do you have so many forks, Gerald?' I asked in morbid wonder.

He shrugged his beautifully broad shoulders where he leaned naked in the doorway, but I could tell my close inspection of his kitchen was making him uncomfortable.

'There must be some reason you have so many forks,' I insisted, inspecting the stove. It looked old.

'So I don't have to wash them every day,' he admitted reluctantly. 'I think I have about a two-month supply.'

I looked at him incredulously. 'And you just let them sit in your sink for two months?'

He shrugged again but stood up straight as if preparing to defend his domestic lethargy. 'I hate housework,' he stated the obvious.

'I can see that, but how can you stand to eat Healthy Choice dinners all the time? They taste like cardboard!'

His mouth hardened obstinately. 'They're all right. You just have to know which ones to buy. I like keeping my fat intake below twenty-two grams a day if possible.'

'What?! Are you kidding me, twenty-two grams of fat per day? You must be joking. That's impossible, we breathe in that much fat everyday.'

'Yes, it is possible.' He crossed his arms stubbornly. 'I've done it.'

'Well, that's ridiculous. A man your size can consume over fifty or sixty grams of fat per day and not gain weight.' I quickly closed the cabinet beneath the sink, which proved to be a graveyard of plastic grocery bags. 'Your body and your skin need natural oils; you can't live off just twenty-two grams of fat per day,' I insisted angrily.

'Well,' he relaxed his combative stance somewhat, 'I have to admit that after a few days I desperately need to have a cheeseburger and fries or something else seriously fattening to feel right.'

I rolled my eyes but refrained from further comment. Once I began cooking for him things would be different. He might gain a few pounds, but overall he would look and be healthier, and generally feel much better as well. I couldn't yet face the thought of having to cook in that kitchen, however; I would cross that bridge when I came to it. I would make the limited space work for me, somehow…

Hand-in-hand (i.e. he pulled me forcibly out of his kitchen before I could further criticize his culinary habits) we walked back out into the black forest of sculptures. I carefully watched my steps across the unpolished wooden floor in case there were any stray modeling tools lying around. I was languidly relaxed enough by how good and hard he had fucked me not to worry about the domestic slavery awaiting me. It was obvious this man could not be tamed into performing household chores on a daily basis, and I had no desire to try and break his spirited resistance to menial tasks. If I wanted to maintain a clean, comfortable, organized living space, I would have to see to it myself, which was fine with me. I performed the same chores living alone, and even though to do them for both of us would double my workload, it would also give me a much greater satisfaction and pleasure than just cleaning and cooking for myself. In fact, Gerald's aversion to housework, and especially to cooking, secretly pleased me because I hate sharing my kitchen with anyone.

'Gerald, my mother is spending the next two days down in Key Biscayne with her… friend, Ernesto, so I'll have the house all to myself.'

He had been pensively studying my clay figure while still holding my flesh-and-blood hand, but now he smiled at me. 'Are you inviting me over for a slumber party, Ariana?'

I slipped my arms around his chest, snuggling up as close as I possibly could to his delicious strength and warmth. 'I think it would be lovely, don't you?'

He hugged me back fiercely. 'Yes, I do!'

CHAPTER TWELVE

Once again I had the pleasure of seeing Gerald completely naked in the kitchen, only this time it was my mother's large state-of-the-art space we were occupying at the beginning of what promised to be a wonderfully hedonistic evening. Earlier that afternoon I had walked home alone in order to prepare my infamous meat lasagna, which was resting on one of the counters covered with tinfoil ready to go into the oven. But first, my artistic lover was going to display another of his talents to me while I watched standing as close to him as I possibly could without interfering with his movements. I had helped him assemble all the necessary tools and ingredients, and he was now ready to show me how to make the perfect Vodka Martini.

CLASSIC VODKA MARTINIS FOR TWO

16 oz of good quality Vodka, ice cold – it will be very slightly viscous at the right temperature

32 oz Stainless Steel Shaker at room temperature

16 ounces of cracked and slightly Crushed Ice – this is important. The ideal is to have a mix of ice comprised mostly of pea-sized pieces and some powder. It's okay to have some bigger pieces mixed in as well, but then you need a little bit more ice.

Crush the ice by wrapping two large handfuls of cubes in a non-fleece kitchen towel and beating it with a large spoon.

1 oz of Italian White Vermouth, cold
A Generous Dash of olive brine from a good bottle of green pimento-stuffed Green Olives
8 jumbo Spanish pimento-stuffed Olives
2 Toothpicks
Two 10 oz martini glasses, chilled

Place the Ice, Vodka, vermouth and Brine in the shaker in that order (otherwise the brine might solidify) then squeeze one whole Olive into the shaker, adding the crushed remains.

Put the lid on and shake vigorously for a few minutes, until a white crust forms on the outside of the shaker. A misty white bloom will form first, then a crust.

Set out the chilled glasses, impale three jumbo Olives onto each toothpick, and place them in the martini glasses.

Pour the contents of the shaker equally into each glass, shaking when necessary to release the liquid trapped in the crushed ice. Now take the remaining Olive and squeeze its juice over the top of each martini. With some practice, beautiful designs can be made on the surface of the martinis with the iridescent olive juice. Admire, then enjoy!

* * *

'm in good company when I try to describe what Gerald's Martini made me feel like: Anais Nin wrote an 'ode' to the Martini while she was on a book tour describing how it transformed her hotel room. I had ordered Vodka Martinis before in a variety of bars, but I had never experienced one as transcendent as Gerald's. He filled two ten-ounce violet-tinted glasses to the brim, decorated the surface of each drink with a spiral of olive juice, then we each carefully carried our glass out into the living room. I had already laid out an appetizer of cold cooked shrimp and cocktail sauce, and there was an X-rated movie in the DVD player, although we would probably enjoy that later. At the moment, we were fully occupied with the highly pleasurable task of sipping our drinks and eating shrimp. That first sip of vodka, on which a slight film of ice had formed, hit my tongue pure as a revelation sensually rooted in the slight tang of the olive brine.

'Oh, My God,' I said, and promptly savored another mouthful of the powerful spirit. There was only a ghost of Vermouth evident, and all it did was intensify the vodka's clarity like the vague memory of a warm Italian spring in Antarctica.

'What do you think?' Gerald asked, his smile indicating he knew the answer but wanted to hear it anyway.

'I think this is the most delicious Martini I've ever tasted in my life!' I took another sip of the enchanted liquid crystal dimension at my fingertips. 'And I'm not just saying that either,' I added fervently. I raised my glass to admire the geometric beauty of the drink, my metaphysical nature pleased by the fact that I was drinking from an inverted glass pyramid.

He set his own glass down on the coffee table before us, and dipped a shrimp into the cocktail sauce. 'These are delicious, too. Thank you, Ariana, this is the best slumber party I've ever been to.'

'Wait until you taste my two-meat lasagna.'

'I can't wait. It'll be perfect. I like having meat after a Martini.'

'Mm, so do I...' I rested my free hand over his relaxed but still enticingly large cock.

He glanced over his shoulder at the front door. 'You're sure your mom's gone for two days?'

'Quite sure.'

'That's nice. Put your drink down and suck my cock.'

I enjoyed my own special appetizer for a few minutes before he let me return to my Martini, which was making me feel better than I could ever remember feeling. It was his company that was doing it enhanced by the ancient art of distilling alcohol from grain, the cradle and the pinnacle of civilization right there in my mother's living room.

'So, do you own a lot of porno movies, Gerald?' The one in the DVD player now had come from his apartment.

'No, just a few quality ones. Antonio Adamo is one of my favorite XXX directors.'

'Well that figures, he's Italian.'

He cast me a mock frown. 'I'm not your mother.'

'I know, I'm just teasing you.' I licked my fingertips after enjoying a particularly succulent shrimp.

'Mm, I love watching you do that,' he murmured, then suddenly cupped my naked breasts in his hands and sucked hungrily on one of my nipples.

'Stop that,' I begged, because he was making my pussy so warm and wet it almost hurt.

'Why, don't you like it?'

'Of course I like it… but I should put the lasagna in the oven, it's going to take an hour.'

'Oh, all right.' He let go of me. 'But hurry back.'

When I returned from the kitchen, I was deep in a disturbing train of thought I wanted to share with him. 'I think it's a mistake to group all forms of pornography together,' I stated as I sat down beside him on the couch again.

'Go on.' He sat back, drink in hand, and listened to me attentively.

'I think that obviously some pornography goes way too far in an unhealthy sense, but not all adult content is so extreme, therefore it shouldn't all be grouped and judged together. Urination as an erotic act, anal sex, fisting, bondage and domination, all these things and more may be shocking to some people, but they're not hurting anyone; they're not evil in the sense that they're violating basic ethical laws and the fabric of society isn't in danger of unraveling because of them. But movies that show a girl being kidnapped and raped by a group of men and then killed, that's wrong; that's evil in the sense that the people who make these movies are trying to divorce sex from reality. In real life it's wrong to force anyone to do something against their will and it's certainly wrong to kill them for your own sick pleasure!'

He put his Martini down. 'Calm down, Ariana, it's all right.' He took my glass from me and set it down next to his. 'Come here.' He drew me close to him. 'I agree with you, there's no justification for films like that.'

'I saw a Front Line special about pornography where they interviewed a couple that makes pretend snuff films,' I wasn't ready to be soothed yet, 'and they weren't all acting. The girl involved didn't really know just how far the men were going to be allowed to go with her. She was actually kicked and beaten and raped on film, and then they pretended to cut her throat at the end! It's wrong to make movies like that just because there's a sick audience for them. Society has every right to pass laws against those kinds of movies. In my opinion, that's the definition of obscenity – something that violates your human rights. Sexual acts aren't obscene just because they involve certain body parts – they're obscene if they're a violation of your sovereign rights as a human being!'

'Yes, that's obvious,' he said mildly.

'Well, it may be obvious to us, but pornography is all grouped together now in a way that's very unhealthy.'

'Yes, I agree.'

'One of the directors of this faux snuff film was actually a woman, and she tried to defend what she did to her friend, the actress in the film, by saying that sometimes it's sexually stimulating to be hit, that it makes your pussy tingle. Can you believe that? I'm sure she realizes there's a big difference between consensual love slaps and being brutally kicked!'

'That's her problem, Ariana. Some people will do anything for money. You shouldn't let it upset you so much.'

'I know I shouldn't, but it's all our problems, really, because movies like that make even me, who knows better, want to take a conservative stand against the adult movie industry.'

'I know, and we don't have to watch that movie tonight, we can just–'

'Oh, but I want to watch it.' I looked up at his face from beneath the warm, safe harbor of his arm. 'I'm all for quality erotica. I'm looking forward to seeing it, really.'

He gazed down at me soberly, concern for my feelings knitting the skin between his eyebrows. 'Are you sure?' he asked gently.

'Yes, I'm sure. I'm sorry, I didn't mean to go on like that, it's just that I started thinking about that Front Line special and getting mad and I wanted to express my feelings to you.'

'Good.' He squeezed my shoulders. 'I want you always to express your feelings to me, Ariana. Do you understand? Never hold anything back from me.'

'I won't,' I sighed. 'I promise.'

* * *

TWO IS BETTER THAN ONE MEAT SAUCE

1/2 lb Lean Ground Beef or Sirloin
1/2 lb Ground Pork
1 Large Spanish Onion, chopped
Basil Olive Oil (or Extra Virgin Olive Oil & Fresh Basil)
3-4 tsp minced Garlic
28 oz can Crushed Tomatoes
Pinch of Sugar
Sea Salt
Freshly Ground Black Pepper
1 tsp Dried Oregano
1/4 cup Fresh Parsley, chopped

Mixing ground beef with ground pork adds a slight sweetness and an intense richness to this sauce I find incomparable. Sure, you can just use one pound of ground beef, but then you won't know what you're missing.

Brown the ground Beef and the ground Pork over high heat in a deep frying pan until just barely cooked through, then carefully drain out the fat before seasoning it liberally with Salt and Pepper before adding the chopped Onion, the Basil Olive Oil and the Garlic. Continue cooking for about five minutes, until the meat is cooked through and the onion is soft and golden.

Add the crushed Tomatoes to the pan, the pinch of Sugar, the Sea Salt, freshly ground Black Pepper and the Oregano. Bring to a boil, then reduce the heat to Low and simmer, covered, for 30 minutes or more, the longer the better. About ten minutes before serving, stir in the fresh Parsley.

Drench your favorite pasta with this hearty sauce and make sure to have freshly grated Parmesan Cheese to go with it. Or, you can make my slightly less sinful, but just as totally fulfilling, Meat Lasagna with it.

LESS SINFUL BUT OH-SO-GOOD LASAGNA

One batch of TWO IS BETTER THAN ONE MEAT SAUCE (see previous recipe)
16 oz container small curd fat-free Cottage Cheese
2 Eggs (I always use organic eggs simply because they taste better)
1 Cup Soy Parmesan Cheese
Sea Salt
Freshly ground Black Pepper
16 oz Package Shredded Mozzarella & Provolone Cheese Mix (or you can use 8oz shredded Mozzarella and 8oz of Six-Cheese Italian Blend (such as Mozzarella, Parmesan, Romano, Provolone, Asiago & Fontina)
1 16 oz Package Oven Ready Lasagna Noodles

Follow the instructions in the preceding recipe for the

Meat Sauce only DO NOT simmer it for half-an-hour before adding the chopped fresh Parsley.

Pre-heat the oven to 350°

In a large bowl beat the Eggs and add the Fat-Free Cottage Cheese and the Soy Parmesan Cheese, stirring well to combine. Season the mixture with some Sea Salt and freshly ground Black Pepper.

In an 8" x 11.5" x 2" glass oven pan, lay out as many of the Lasagna Noodles as needed to cover. Top them with 1/3 of the Meat Sauce, then 1/2 of the Cottage Cheese mixture, and finally sprinkle a generous layer of the shredded Mozzarella and Provolone on top. Repeat the process two more times, finishing off with the Meat Sauce and the Shredded Cheese. Dust the top with some more Soy Parmesan Cheese and very carefully cover the pan with tin foil, tenting it to make sure the layer of cheese does not stick to it when it begins melting.

Bake in a 350° oven for 40 minutes, discard the foil and bake an additional 15 minutes. Remove the pan from the oven and let stand for 15 minutes. This Lasagna refrigerates and freezes very nicely. Re-heat any leftovers in a 300° oven covered with foil until heated through.

TOFU FETTUCCINI ALFREDO

1 18 oz Package Soft Tofu
1/2 Cup Organic Chicken Broth
1/2 Cup Heavy Cream

2 Tbls Butter, at room temperature
1/2 Cup Soy Parmesan Cheese
1/2 Cup Italian Cheese blend (Mozarella, Provolone, Parmesan, Romano, Asiago & Fontina)
1 1/2 tsp Sea Salt
Freshly ground Black Pepper, to taste
16 oz Fettuccini Noodles, cooked and drained

While you cook the Fettuccini, puree the Tofu in a microwave-safe bowl, then stir in the Chicken Broth, the Heavy Cream and the Sea Salt.

Microwave the Tofu, Broth and Cream mixture on high, covered, for 2-3minutes (depends on how powerful your microwave is) add the Butter and the grated Cheeses, and microwave, covered, for another 2-3 minutes.

Sprinkle a generous amount of freshly grated Black Pepper over the sauce, and ladle it over the cooked Fettuccini noodles. Serve at once with a pepper mill. This recipe serves two very generously and is considerably lower in fat not to mention healthier than traditional Fettuccini Alfredo, yet I find it to be just as rich and sinfully satisfying. You can top the pasta with sautéed chicken breast chunks (see TOFU CAESAR SALAD DRESSING) or even better with oven-grilled Shrimp before pouring the white sauce on top.

OVEN-GRILLED SHRIMP

Peeled tail-on or tail-off Medium-sized Shrimp
Rosemary Olive Oil

Sea Salt
Freshly Ground Black Pepper
Dried Oregano
Fresh Parsley
Cooking Spray

Preheat the Broiler while you toss the Shrimp with the Rosemary Olive Oil, the Salt, Pepper, Oregano and Parsley. (Or better yet, let the Shrimp marinate for an hour or two.) I won't give exact measurements here; use as much of these ingredients as feels right for the amount of shrimp you'll be cooking.

Spray a Non-Stick Cookie Sheet with the Cooking Spray, spread the Shrimp evenly across it, and broil them about 5 minutes each side. Watch them carefully; you don't want to overcook them. They should be golden brown on the outside but still plump and juicy on the inside.

CHAPTER THIRTEEN

Even though it may sound kinky, it was beyond wonderful sharing my childhood bedroom and bed with Gerald. Naturally the mattress had been replaced several times, but it was still the corner of space where I had lain as a little girl dreaming of true love determined to find my soul mate when I grew up. Now this space was inhabited by my adult body and the body of the man who was so far doing a very good job of making all my dreams come true. He had also made me come more than once before we finally slipped beneath the covers together, wonderfully felled by vodka, lasagna, wine and sex.

It was wonderful sharing my bed with Gerald, especially falling asleep in his arms with my head resting against his chest, but that's not to say it wasn't also a bit of a trial. I sleep deeply and dream constantly (so much so that until I met my beautiful sculptor waking up was often a disappointment in light of all my exciting nocturnal adventures) and toss and turn a lot at night. With this very special man lying in my bed, I didn't sleep as well as I normally do because I had to make an effort not to move around too much and disturb him. As a result I lay awake for long stretches at a time debating how long to wait before shifting positions again, judging by his breathing how deeply asleep he was and if my motion would disturb him or not. I also lay awake thinking about the fact that commonly accepted rules of long-term relationships often contribute to the difficulty many people seem to have in staying together. I decided when the time was right I would take the subject up with Gerald about sleeping in separate beds when we moved in together. I reasoned that just because you love someone profoundly and want to spend the rest of your life with them doesn't mean you need to be condemned to sleeping next to them every night worrying about disturbing them, and as a consequence not getting enough rest yourself, which in turn puts unnecessary pressure on you and robs you of your full energy, therefore probably making you grouchy... the domino effect of the seemingly innocent rule couples should sleep in the same bed struck me as rather ghastly as I lay there pondering all the potential negative repercussions. I also decided if our finances permitted it would be a good idea to have separate bathrooms as well, a very good idea. I concluded true love and logical thinking should not cancel each other out like matter and anti-matter, but rather they should work together to create a whole other, much better universe than traditionally conceived possible.

At one point during that long but wonderfully fulfilling and constructive night, I finally fell asleep for good. I awoke an indeterminate amount of time later to the sweet singing of birds in the trees outside my windows, although if the truth be told it sounded more like a cacophony as incessantly chirped messages urgently communicating the whereabouts of succulent worms and flowers annoyingly disturbed my restful slumber. The noise made by the poetically idealized feathery army woke me up, and kept me up even though my room was still dark thanks to the abundant foliage surrounding it, which proved a double-edged sword since it was also incredibly noisy with life. I turned over onto my side and lay there contentedly for a while gazing at Gerald's sleeping profile or at least what I could see of it. He had one of my pillows draped over his eyes and the top of his head, and he would obviously have buried himself beneath it if he hadn't also needed to keep breathing. He lay on his back with the cotton jersey sheet pulled all he way up to his chin, his hands clutching it like a little boy determined not to have it snatched away by some nameless nocturnal enemy. I smiled imagining all the myriad of little endearing things I would discover about him over time. His nose and mouth were beautifully shaped, truly statuesque, as was the rest of his firm but also deliciously tender physique. It was as if the depth of his being and compassion were embodied in his skin, which was softer than the skin of any man I had ever been with and yet not at all delicate or effeminate. God is keeping his mortal clay nice and moist and supple, I thought, and He made this man especially for me, just as all my unique thoughts and feelings and sensations were mysteriously made especially for him...

The high-pitched chirping of happy birds continued wreaking sentimental havoc with my mental synapses for about thirty minutes before I finally decided to get up and shower while my handsome soul mate slept for however long he felt like it.

In the bathroom, I turned on the hot water thinking about another relationship myth in need of dispelling – that lovers always shower together and enjoy having sex while they do so. In my opinion sex in the tub can definitely be fun, but it is also, I feel, highly overrated. In my book it ranks right down there with trite games such as covering your lover with whipped cream, then licking it off. It seems to me you need to love whipped cream much more than the person underneath it since the sugary taste of chemicals overrides the more subtle flavor of bare flesh.

I was intensely happy (if a touch cranky and unsympathetic in my thinking) on that beautiful sunny morning in May in my air conditioned bathroom in already brutally hot south Florida. When I returned to my bedroom, temptingly wrapped in an innocent white towel, I was somewhat disappointed to find Gerald still buried beneath a pillow and showing no signs of life whatsoever. I wandered idly over to my dresser, where a morbid curiosity made me pick up my cell phone and carry it out into the living room. The shrill beep that resounded through the silent house when I switched it on told me I had a voicemail message, and I dreaded it. I had not forgotten Eric's promise to call me again to see if I had changed my mind about seeing him, and sure enough, I recognized his number on the Received Calls display. It was a relief to discover he had not actually left a message, which I hoped meant he had given up on me. The fact that I was not answering my phone should tell him I had not changed my mind and was beyond the possibility of him talking me into doing so.

Switching off my electronic butler again, I returned to the bedroom, and this time was delighted to see Gerald was awake, if just barely; at least the pillow was no longer over his eyes.

'What time is it?' he asked so quietly I barely heard him.

'Nine o'clock,' I replied cheerfully, perching on the edge of the bed and smiling down at him.

'Why are you wearing that towel?' he demanded after a moment; it had taken his sleepy brain cells that long to register the affront.

I promptly stood up and discarded the damp terrycloth.

He flung the sheet off his naked body. 'Come here.'

I snuggled happily next to him, but apparently he didn't just want me to lie beside him because he placed one of his hands gently on my head, and urged my face down towards his cock. 'Wake me up,' he commanded, and I gladly took his already semi-stiff penis between my lips. My mouth was slightly dry, so I concentrated on sucking his head for a minute, holding firmly onto his shaft to lubricate it with my saliva with the first sweet taste of his semen as he responded to my ministrations. It pleased me how quickly I was able to make him hard, and occasionally I opened my eyes as I sucked him to admire the beautiful cock in my mouth. The soft sounds of pleasure he emitted every now and then assured me I was doing a good job of pleasing him as well as myself. I kept up a steady rhythm of stroking him with my fist and swallowing him whole, alternating between caressing his head with the inside of my cheek and the more stimulating entrance to my throat.

When he finally sat up and urged me onto my hands and knees, I was more than ready for his hard thrust from behind. With my cheek pressed against the bed, I arched my back and offered him full, unrestrained access to my sex; assuming a position in which he could plunge all the way into my slick pussy. He fucked me fast and deep, until all I had to do was reach down and touch my clitoris to start coming. He didn't say a word, utterly focused on his penetrations as I consciously used my vaginal muscles to squeeze his cock, thrilling myself with my power to grip and caress his erection with my deepest self. I milked his deliciously rigid penis from the base to the head with a ripple-like motion of my innermost flesh I could feel was irresistible to him. The sensation of him beginning to climax combined with the urgent motion of my fingertips stimulated my clitoris so much I was able to orgasm with him, an incomparable experience beyond description.

* * *

Those two days were so lovely I can hardly remember anything about them except how happy I was; how utterly relaxed and content with the present as well as excited about the future. We spent some time in his studio again (I couldn't quite think of it as an apartment/living space yet) but he didn't really get much work done since I spent most of the time I was there re-evaluating my opinion of waterbeds. I avoided his kitchen like the plague, for the time being suppressing this major little glitch in my joy. I knew in my soul beyond a shadow of a doubt that Gerald and I were destined to be sinfully happy together, and my culinary self took heart and waited to see just how things would work out. That I could never be really happy cooking in such a little old kitchen was a fact, but now more than ever I had confidence in the Magic Pattern, and I relaxed in its mysterious arms as absolutely as I relaxed in Gerald's ardent yet tender embrace.

I lived on the Bay in Boston, but it had been a long time since I spent time just relaxing in front of the ocean, so we took my rental car down to Key Biscayne, and spent part of the afternoon sprawled out on a big towel in between body surfing in the invigoratingly cold waves. This was a dangerous sport for me; the powerful rush of the tide kept threatening to rip off both the top and bottom halves of my red Brazilian bikini, which I think is what Gerald most enjoyed about the activity. He smiled appreciatively every time the ocean innocently succeeded in stripping me for an instant.

'I should have worn my black one-piece!' I gasped after a particularly rough landing in the gritty sand where a huge wave violently flung me, and of course I had loved every violent second of it.

'I'm glad you didn't,' he said as he helped me adjust my spaghetti-thin shoulder straps.

We enjoyed taking turns caressing suntan lotion all over each other, but there were too many people around, especially children, for us to enjoy lingering too long under the sun. It was late in the afternoon when Gerald helped me back into my sarong and we walked contentedly back to the car.

We didn't drive straight back to my mom's house. We stopped at the Rusty Pelican for a refreshing drink. The sun was beginning to set as I ordered a glass of Chardonnay. We sat at a table beside the floor-to-ceiling windows looking west over the Bay towards downtown Miami, the city into which the earth's fiery lord appeared to be gradually sinking.

'I'll have a Sapphire and tonic, a single in a tall glass,' Gerald told the waitress, looking steadily up into her eyes from his comfortable chair to make sure she understood him correctly. 'With a slice of lime, please.'

It was a lovely place and time of day to sit and talk for a while. Every muscle in my body, and every emotion in my personality, was so relaxed the world felt enchanted in a very real way transcending any fantasy. The wine seemed to capture the golden light sparkling across the water inside my glass as every sip filled me with a growing sense of magic existing at my fingertips if I truly believed in it. The restaurant was artificially cold, but even the slight chill I suffered wet-haired and bare-shouldered in my damp sarong was sensually enjoyable to me as I listened attentively to what Gerald was saying while admiring the way his eyes both absorbed and reflected the dying light. Every now and then boats sailed or motored by outside the glass as the water darkened, the sky grew more luminous, and the distant city began coming to life as if powered by the sun descending behind the buildings. It was in those moments, as Gerald and I both fell quiet, that I let go of Boston in my heart and embraced the thought of moving back to Miami. My mother and all my other relatives would be ecstatic because I had made it clear to them I would never ever come back to Miami. God was having a little fun with me, but I didn't care. In fact, if this was the way Providence amused itself, I was all for being played with.

* * *

Even though I tried to insist, Gerald refused to let me cook that night. After we got cleaned up (and yes, that time we showered together, shampooing each other's hair and lingering with the soap in all those luscious areas to make sure they were completely sand-free) I slipped on a lavender sundress over clean white socks and sneakers, transferred all my essentials from a black purse to a white one, and together we set off on foot in search of a restaurant. We had debated whether or not to head out to South Beach and all the restaurants on Lincoln Road, but in the end the pleasure of walking leisurely hand-in-hand won out over dealing with traffic, then being forced to drive home inebriated, for there was no question of not having wine with dinner.

We ended up at an infamous old Cuban restaurant La Havana Vieja mainly because I had heard it was under new management and I was hoping the quality of the cuisine had improved. It hadn't, not noticeably, but even though I preferred my own cooking, the company was more than good enough to make up for the lack of intense gastronomic delight.

At some point during the lackluster meal, Gerald announced quietly, 'I have a feeling something very good is going to happen soon.'

'Is going to happen?' I teased.

'You're not just something good, Ariana, you're magnificent.'

'Thank you.' I looked away shyly for an instant before meeting his eyes again curiously. 'So, what do you think is going to happen?'

'I think my friend from the gallery is planning to arrange something,' he replied, and kept eating.

'Arrange what?' I asked urgently, sensing that whatever it was would affect our future together, which had become from the moment I met him the all-important topic in my life now and forever.

'I think he's going to give me my own show next month.' It was his turn to look away humbly for a moment.

'Oh, my God, that's wonderful!' I exclaimed as quietly as the Cuban half of my nature permitted. 'Your own show, with just your pieces in the gallery?'

'That's usually what having your own show implies.' The expression in his eyes as he looked into mine belied his sarcastic reply. 'And if I could sell just two or three of my pieces during that show… well, let's just say it would enable me to execute my master plan, which I intend to begin setting in motion tomorrow.'

'Your master plan?' I was suddenly so excited I had to put my fork down and stop eating. Just to hear him say 'master plan' turned me on so much I could hardly tolerate the suspense.

'Yes. I'm meeting with my friend tomorrow afternoon, the one who owns the gallery, then I'm seeing a few other people tomorrow night and Thursday night. I'll let you know how it all goes.'

My heart sank. 'Then I won't see you again until Friday night?' I knew I sounded spoiled and petulant, but I couldn't help it.

He smiled at me with a tenderness that only made me more desperate not to lose sight of him; when we weren't together, part of me was almost afraid I was only imagining he existed. 'We still have tonight and tomorrow morning,' he reminded me, 'and by then you'll be so exhausted you'll be glad of the rest.'

'Oh, really? Exhausted from what?' I prompted.

He leaned over the table towards me. 'Exhausted by how long and hard I'm going to fuck you.'

'Mm,' I smiled as I sipped my wine, but there was a slight thorn in my contentment I couldn't help worrying over even though I despised myself for it. 'Who else are you going to see besides your friend who owns the gallery?' I tried to make the question sound innocent and casual, but it turned out sounding exactly like what it was – a jealous probe.

'Let's just say I have some divesting to do.'

I was grateful he concentrated on his food and chose to ignore my pathetic lapse in trust. My faith in this man was already so profound there really was no excuse for it.

'It's all part of my master plan, Ariana,' he added, meeting my eyes with an intense determination that made him look even more handsome than usual. 'If things go well, as I have a feeling they will, we'll celebrate Friday night.'

'You're not going to tell me your plan?' I pouted.

'No, not yet,' he said firmly. 'I don't want you getting your hopes up until I'm sure it's all going to work out the way I want it to. Now finish your dinner like a good girl and let's go home.'

Let's go home… coming from his lips the sound of those words was sweeter than anything my soul had ever tasted.

* * *

The next day, Gerald left at around one o'clock in the afternoon and, true to his word, he left me deliciously worn out enough that I didn't miss him painfully, only enough to cherish the sweet temporary heartache of his absence. It was intolerably hot outside, and there was nowhere I needed to go, so I stayed at home and faced what I had been avoiding – my laptop and all the e-mails I knew would be crowding my Inbox. I set the computer up out on the coffee table in the living room, where I could sit barefoot on the carpet Japanese style wearing an old grey tank-top and shorts both dangerously close to disintegrating in the next wash, but they were my most beloved comfortable house clothes and I would wear them to the very end.

I was relieved not to find any urgent e-mails requiring my immediate response. My whole being was so relaxed I found it nearly impossible to get back into work-mode just yet. Before I flew down to Florida, I had been paid for three separate articles at once and made a nice fat deposit in my bank account. Or at least it had seemed that way, but now that the expense of a cross-country move loomed before me, my finances looked considerably less cushy. So profound was my contentment, however, that I couldn't bring myself to worry about that or anything else. We had not actually discussed it yet, but I knew that from now on Gerald and I would always take care of each other in every sense. Even if he became a fabulously famous and wealthy sculptor, I had no intention of letting him support me, but the painfully sharp edge had been taken off my circumstances and I knew it. I no longer had to worry about surviving all on my own.

I had just closed my lap-top with a satisfied click when I heard the sound of a car out in the driveway. Mami was back from Key West. I went to open the door for her, and smiled at Ernesto striding up the walkway ahead of her carrying one of her designer Italian suitcases.

'Hola, Ari,' he greeted me with his characteristic cheerfulness. 'How are you, sweety?'

'I've never been better,' I replied truthfully, moving aside so he could walk in and put down the suitcase. 'Mami, you got a tan!' The delicate way the pale skin of her cheeks and nose had burned made her look ten years younger, and that was saying a lot since she already looked great for her age.

Ay, por Dios!' she scoffed. 'I got burned is what I got.'

I smiled at her indulgently as we hugged and kissed affectionately. 'Did you have a nice time anyway, I hope?'

'It was wonderful,' she admitted with a secret little smile, and said no more.

Ernesto and I looked at each other in astonishment. The only time mami ever said something was wonderful without adding a qualifying string of dissatisfied 'buts' was after returning from one of her countless trips to Italy. It was such a special moment, I decided not to wait to make my grand announcement. 'I'm moving back down to Miami,' I blurted, and Ernesto's chocolate-brown eyes grew even bigger as he looked at Rosa in happy anticipation of her ecstatic reaction.

Mami closed the door behind her before turning back to face me and asking very calmly, 'What did you just say?'

'I'm moving down to Miami.'

She blinked at me a few times then glanced at Ernesto, but he was no help; he just stood there with his arms crossed over his chest savoring her emotional reactions like a heady beverage he was helplessly fond of. 'Would the handsome Italian sculptor we had over for dinner the other night have something to do with this sudden decision of yours, Ari? Don't you think it's a little soon to... to make such an important decision?' She was making a painful effort not to let her selfish excitement at my announcement override her maternal responsibilities.

'Oh, mami, stop it!' I impatiently put her out of her misery. 'You know it's not too soon, you met him, you felt him and me together. He's my soul mate, mami, there's no doubt about it in my heart or in my soul, and he feels the same way about me.'

'Ay, Ari!' She handed the grinning Ernesto her Italian leather purse and hugged me with as much strength as she possessed. 'I'm so happy! Wait until I tell your grandfather! Wait until I tell the Sorianos, and Claudio, and Lourdes and...' The list went on and on, but at least – respectful of my fiercely independent spirit and bad temper when I'm pressured into doing anything – she carefully refrained from calling any of them 'guests' and even going near the word 'wedding'. But I knew my mother; she wasn't about to settle for one blessing when she could have another, and I sighed to think what I was getting myself into returning to the familial fold as Ernesto winked at me sympathetically.

* * *

That night I cooked for mami, myself and Ernesto. Keeping busy in the kitchen was a good way to take my mind off how much I already missed Gerald.

We've all had Mexican-style burritos, but I highly recommend trying these for a savory change of pace.

MY CUBAN BURRITOS

1 lb Ground Pork
Juice of One Lime
Sea Salt
Freshly Ground Black Pepper
Ground Thyme
Minced Oregano
Powdered Garlic
1 16 oz can Cuban-style Black Beans (such as Kirby or Goya) drained

4 Medium (burrito-sized) Flour Tortillas (I use Spinach-Basil tortillas)
2 Tomatoes, cut, seeded and diced
Extra Sharp Cheddar Cheese, grated
Light Sour Cream

While cooking the ground Pork over high heat, season it with the Lime Juice, the Sea Salt, freshly ground Black Pepper, a generous sprinkling of the ground Thyme, the Oregano and the powdered Garlic. Make sure the Pork is completely cooked through before removing it from the pan with a slotted spoon to drain out the fat.

Preheat the oven to 350°. Lay out each flour Tortilla on a cutting board or on a large plate. Using a soup spoon, vertically line the center of each Tortilla with 1/4 of the cooked Pork, and then add 1/4 can of the Black Beans to each one. Now fold the bottom and top halves of the Tortillas over the mixture, fold in the sides, and quickly turn them over.

Carefully transfer the filled Tortillas to a non-stick oven pan lightly coated with Cooking Spray and bake them, loosely covered with tin foil, for 15 minutes, then discard the foil and bake them for another 5 minutes while also heating two oven-safe plates in the oven.

Put two of the Pork Burritos on each plate, cover the top of each one with a thin layer of Light Sour Cream, top with a generous sprinkling of Extra Sharp Cheddar Cheese, and finish off the with the diced tomatoes.

Serve at once. This recipe feeds two heartily and four modestly and is fabulous accompanied by Fried Green Plantains if you're lucky enough to be able to find them in your supermarket. If not, they are usually always sold in Latin grocery stores, and even though they are deep-fried, it's still one of my favorite ways of adding Potassium to my diet.

FRIED GREEN PLANTAINS

2 large Green Plantains
Canola Oil
One Brown Bag
Sea Salt

Fill a large frying pan with about one inch of Canola Oil and heat on medium-high.

With a sharp knife, slice the skin of each plantain from end to end and then carefully peel it off. If the plantain is still nice and green and firm, the skin will come off easily.

Chop each plantain into one inch pieces, turn the heat down to low, and very gently deep-fry them for 3-5 minutes on each side. The goal here is to get them soft and golden but not to brown them; that comes later. Remove to a plate covered with a paper towel.

Now, one at a time, place the plantain pieces on a brown bag, then fold the bag over it and crush it with the base of your palm to about ? inch in thickness. After all the plantain pieces are flattened, you can refrigerate them covered with a paper towel until you're ready to serve dinner. Then all you need to do is heat the oil again on high (use the same oil you cooked them in the first time) and fry the plantain slices in two batches until they're a nice golden-brown; you don't want them too dark. Drain them on a plate covered with a paper towel and immediately sprinkle them generously with Sea Salt.

This recipe is not as time-consuming or complicated as it might sound. In fact, it's really quite quick and easy. It's also one of the only Cuban recipes my grandmother actually ever taught me.

SINLESS TURKEY CHILI

2 lbs Ground Turkey Breast (this is nearly fat free and not to be confused with regular ground turkey)
1 large Spanish onion, chopped
2 tsp minced Garlic
1 Tbls Extra Virgin Olive Oil
1 Tbls Butter
2 Tbls Chili Powder
1 16 oz can crushed Tomatoes
2 16 oz cans spicy Chili Beans
1 1/2 tsp Sea Salt
1 tsp Sugar
1/3 cup Dry Red Wine
1 large Bay Leaf
Freshly Ground Black Pepper (just a little)

In a large soup pan, cook the Onion and Garlic in the Olive Oil and Butter for about three minutes, then add the Ground Turkey and cook, covered and stirring every few minutes, until the meat is no longer pink, seasoning it with the 2 Tbls of Chili Powder, the Sea Salt and a little freshly ground Black Pepper.

Turn the heat up to high, add the remaining ingredients to the pan except for the Bay Leaf, and stir well to blend thoroughly. Toss in the Bay Leaf, bring the mixture to a light boil, reduce the heat to medium, then cover and cook for 45 minutes, stirring occasionally.

After 45 minutes, reduce the heat to Low and simmer the chili for another hour or two, the longer the better, stirring every half-hour or so to make sure the mixture doesn't stick to the bottom of the pan. (If the mixture looks dry, feel free to add a little water.)

This recipe makes enough for plenty of left over batches of chili you can keep in your freezer for a quick healthy dinner. Believe it or not, it tastes even better after it's been frozen. I like to serve my chili with organic corn chips, diced tomatoes, extra sharp cheddar cheese and light sour cream, but it's also great over rice or accompanied by corn bread.

CHAPTER FOURTEEN

Gerald called me at around noon on Friday to tell me all was going well and to ask me to meet him at his place at seven o'clock that evening.

It was a very pleasant walk from mami's house to my lover's apartment. I had gone for a twenty-minute jog earlier that morning so my legs were nicely stretched out and all of me felt energized. I had spent part of the afternoon making a list of all the things I wanted to bring down with me from Boston, and even though I had not asked for her help, mami had offered her firm opinion on certain items I should and shouldn't keep; we had argued loudly and happily sitting together at the kitchen table. In the end I hadn't taken her advice on anything, but she hadn't really expected me to – she simply enjoyed giving it. Her budding romance with Ernesto was mellowing her out in all the right places, and I for one was happy the man in my mother's life was someone I had known and liked for years. It made it easier for me to accept him into our intimate fold. Naturally, the list of things I was bringing down with me was ten times longer than the list of things I planned to leave behind. Gerald and I would need to rent a rather large truck, then I would have to put some things into storage in mami's garage, but such was life. Two of the items she tried desperately to get me to leave behind were my exercise bike and weight lifting center, although she agreed I had to keep the bamboo folding screens I hid them behind for aesthetic reasons. It worried me a little the only exercise my mother had ever done in her life was walk, but at least walk she did. She, on the other hand, could not understand the use of exercise equipment; she considered it unnatural and much too boring to be part of a real human being's life. 'After all, Italians aren't obsessed with going to the gym yet none of them are fat and they eat whatever they want to. And you know why? Because all their food comes fresh from the farm, there's no processed junk food or fast food–'

'Shut-up, mami, I'm trying to think.'

'Anyway, that ghastly equipment weighs too much. You can't possibly bring it down with you.'

'Oh, yes I can, and I'm storing it in your garage for a while.'

'What?! You are not–'

'Yes, I am.'

'And how long is a while, if I might ask?'

'Until Gerald and I move into a bigger place together.'

'And how long will that be?'

'It could be years,' I admitted.

'Years?!'

'Or sooner. It all depends on how well his show goes at the gallery.'

'I can't wait to see his work!' I had successfully deflected her train of thought away from my bulky exercise equipment. 'Can't you describe on of his pieces to me?'

'No, you have to see them, but I'm warning you, his work is rather… erotic.'

'Ay, por Dios, I'm a grown woman, Ariana. Do you think Ernesto and I spent the whole time in Key West just petting Hemingway's cats?'

'Mami!' I gasped, then we both laughed happily.

That evening I found Gerald's building without any problems, and my heart seemed to beat itself up a little closer to my throat as I climbed the steps up to his top floor apartment. I suspected from the tone of his voice when he phoned me earlier that his master plan had not encountered any obstacles, and now that I was about to find out what it was, I felt I couldn't wait another second. I knocked politely on his door and stood restlessly on the landing, anxious for some response from within. 'Come in!' he called at last.

The bay windows faced west, and I paused on the threshold in awe. The sunset's golden light was bathing the forest of black statues, flowing between the sensually entranced figures in luminous shafts that made me feel as though all the lovers in the room were about to be released from their spell. Then I saw my own flesh-and-blood lover sitting at a small black wrought-iron table he had placed next to the central window overlooking the treetops. There was a bottle of champagne and two champagne flutes on the table before him, and I did not hesitate to walk over and take my place in the empty iron chair across from his, setting my purse on the floor.

'Good evening, Ariana,' he said, and his smile struck me as triumphant and possessive and everything I had ever dreamed of a man's smile looking like.

'Good evening, Gerald. This is a cute little table. Where did you get it?'

'It was out on the back porch when I moved in. The chairs aren't the most comfortable things on earth, but I wanted us to have a view of the sunset while we toasted our future together.'

'It's all totally lovely!'

'I don't normally drink thirty-dollar bottles of champagne,' he picked it up and placed it between his thighs (an enviable position) 'for the simple reason that I've discovered quite a few equally excellent bottles for under ten dollars, but this was a special occasion.'

I gasped as the cork popped up and hit the ceiling with a sound like a gunshot. 'The suspense is killing me, Gerald! Did you get your show?'

'Of course I got my show.' He smiled as he slowly poured some of the bubbling pearly liquid into my glass. I thought it was going to overflow, but he had judged the level of the foam just right.

'That's wonderful, but that was only part of your master plan, right?'

'Right.' He raised his glass and I quickly followed suit. 'To us,' he said.

'To us,' I echoed.

'And to la dolce vita,' he added before taking a sip. 'Do you like it?'

'Yes, it's wonderful.' I studied the bright orange label. 'Vueve Cliquot Ponsardin,' I read out loud. 'I'm afraid I don't know much about champagne.' I took another appreciative sip, controlling my impatience. He was deliberately keeping me in suspense about his master plan and making me feel helplessly excited, which I suspected was how he liked me. 'It's beautiful here,' I remarked. On my left were the tree tops and the sunset, on my right was the small forest of statues. Yet could I really live here? A home also had to be cozy and possess certain basic amenities, like a couch and a television, not to mention a place to put them, and I wasn't even going to think about the kitchen…

'I spoke to my landlord today, Ariana.'

'Yes?'

'Would you like to hear what he said?'

'Gerald!'

He laughed. 'I told him about you, and about my upcoming show, and I made him realize it would only benefit him in the end if he let me fix up the place.'

'What do you mean fix up the place?' I echoed, scarcely daring to let myself hope.

'Well,' he sipped his champagne with maddening calm, 'if my show goes well it will free up a lot of space in here, and in the future I can arrange to have my completed pieces stored elsewhere.'

'Oh, but I love this little forest of statues,' I declared, already missing them.

'That's very sweet of you, dear.' He reached across the table and caressed the hair out of my eye. 'But we need to make room for us in here now.'

I couldn't argue with that, so I remained happily silent waiting for him to continue.

'The first thing I plan to do is expand and completely remodel the kitchen. You'll be in charge of selecting the new appliances, and once I've determined how big it can be, we can sit down and design it together.'

'Gerald,' I set my glass down, 'it would cost a fortune to hire someone to gut and rebuild the kitchen, contractors are notorious for–'

'Ariana, you weren't listening carefully. I'm going to be doing the construction work, and our gracious landlord is splitting the cost of the materials with us. As for whatever appliances you choose, he's paying for them in full since they'll stay here when we move out in the future, at which point he'll be able to charge an exorbitant amount of rent for this place.'

'You'll be doing the construction work?' I couldn't believe it; I had never met a man who could actually build or fix anything himself even though I knew such creatures existed in theory.

'Why do you look so astonished, Ariana?'

'Because I… um, because I…'

'You know how good I am with my hands.' He smiled and drained his glass.

I did the same, and held it out for him to refill.

'I grew up playing around in my uncle's shop,' he explained. 'Jerry was an excellent carpenter. He taught me a lot, the rest,' he shrugged, 'I picked up myself.'

'I should have known…' I shook my head in giddy disbelief.

'Should have known what?' he asked mildly.

'That you could build me my dream kitchen! You've made all my other dreams come true, why not that one?'

'Why not, indeed?' He chimed his glass against mine again. 'Here's to all our dreams coming true.'

'I'll drink to that.'

'I'm hoping you have some furniture up in Boston you'll be bringing down with you?'

'Oh, yes.'

'Good, because once our friends here are gone,' he glanced fondly at his stone orgy, 'there'll be plenty of room to comfortably accommodate the living. I'm thinking we can put up a dividing wall right about here, and then another one over there to create a little foyer when you walk into the apartment, because the living area should adjoin the bedroom, which means it has to be behind us. There are actually two bedrooms, you know. I didn't show you the other small back room because it's full of boxes and junk. I'll have to do some more divesting.'

'Do you think you could knock down the wall between the two rooms and create one big bedroom?'

'I don't see why not.'

'That would be wonderful, because I really don't want to give up my bed.'

'You don't have to give up anything you don't want to, Ariana,' he said soberly.

'And yet I would give up everything just to be with you, Gerald.'

We chimed glasses again in silence as the room darkened. The sun had disappeared behind one of the old buildings across the street, but our champagne sparkled and flowed like liquid light between our lips as we smiled into each other's eyes.

'Oh, damn!' He set down his glass and stood up abruptly. 'I almost forgot.'

'Forgot what?' I watched him stride through his forest of statues into the miserable little kitchen that would soon be history. Oh, what great pleasure it would give me to help him destroy it!

'I almost forgot this.' He returned carrying a plate he set on the table.

'Oh, my, strawberries and cream, and champagne.' I promptly picked up one of the juicy red berries and dipped it into the little glass bowl filled with cream. 'You're going to seriously spoil me, Gerald.'

'Good.'

'And I fully intend to spoil you, too.'

He discarded the leafy green end of a strawberry. 'I have a feeling I'm going to gain some weight.'

'Maybe a little, but you'll still look great, and life is too short not to enjoy it to the fullest worrying about a couple of extra pounds here and there. I don't believe people have to look like models to be beautiful and sexy; so much of it is about their aura as well as their bone structure.'

'I agree wholeheartedly. After we finish our champagne, I'm going to give you that full body massage you've been craving.'

I gazed at him in wonder. 'And here I thought the evening couldn't possibly get any better!'

'Things can always get better no matter how good they are already, it's called growing, and it's an essential part of human nature.'

'Uh-huh.' I stared at him worshipfully. Everything he said made him look even more handsome to me than he already did. It was going to be a glorious task getting used to being with a man who kept giving me every indication he was even deeper and smarter than I considered myself to be.

It didn't take us long to empty the black stoneware plate of the vivid red strawberries, and with a glass of champagne in hand, we strolled into his bedroom. (It took a while to get there because I kept pausing to admire his naughty artwork.) He had already spread a large forest-green towel across his black comforter and lit four slate-colored candles set in beautiful large brass candleholders.

'Take off your clothes,' he instructed.

For lack of a better place to put it, I set my glass down on the floor, then it was an easy matter to slip off my red cotton tank dress and to slip off my sneakers and socks, which only left my black bikini panties. He had left the room to fetch something, and I deliberately waited for him to return before I slowly slipped my panties down my legs as he watched.

'Mm, the hardest thing about giving you a massage, Ariana, is going to be resisting the desire to fuck you before I'm finished. Lie down on the towel, please, face down.'

I obeyed him gladly, enjoying the way the mattress undulated beneath my naked body as he joined me on the bed. It excited me to feel him kneeling behind me, and I shuddered in delight beneath the sensation of oil trickling down my spine. Yet it was nothing compared to the deep warm pleasure I experienced a moment later when his strong hands began kneading the tension-filled area just below my neck and between my shoulder-blades.

'Oh, my God,' I moaned as his thumbs dug into my muscles and made me aware of painful pockets of tension I hadn't realized were there.

'Is that too hard?' he asked quietly.

'No, it's perfect...' Already it was an effort to speak. Everywhere his breathtakingly talented hands pressed and caressed me hurt and yet also felt better than I would have dreamed possible. Then he discovered a muscle in my upper arms that was so profoundly sore I emitted a little scream of agony when he began gently kneading it with both hands.

'You lift weights,' he said.

'Yes, a little... oh, my God... no, don't stop, please, it hurts, but it also feels unbelievable...' The massage he gave me was in many instances a perfect expression of how pain and ecstasy can sometimes go hand-in-hand as my muscles were utterly unable to distinguish between them. By the time he instructed me to turn around and lie on my back, I was so exquisitely relaxed thinking felt like trying to run through quicksand. The only time I can almost shut off my thoughts and achieve a mysteriously visual meditative state is when I am being massaged. I thought it was all over when he began caressing my breasts, but from there he moved down to my thighs, where I discovered yet another excruciatingly sensitive muscle in their soft inner flesh. He had already ascertained while he was working on the back of my legs that I was a runner, and now he concentrated on the sides of my knees in a way that had me moaning for mercy even as I never wanted him to stop.

It seemed at once too soon and a blissful eternity later when that glorious massage ended. I felt him get off the bed, and opened my eyes to the dreamy vision of him pulling off his shirt, then pushing down his jeans. His cock leapt out fully erect and I licked my lips in anticipation of the internal massage I was about to get. Still lying languidly on my back, I raised my arms over my head as I spread my legs, and my hips rose to meet him on a wave as he quickly knelt on the bed and thrust his rigid penis into my slick hole, making me gasp as his hard-on selfishly forced my pussy open around it. He groaned, sucking hungrily on one of my nipples as he kept jamming his erection as far up inside me as was physically possible, and his head must have been kissing my G-spot because, unbelievably, I felt myself starting to come around him. I eagerly slipped my hand between us, and he helpfully lifted himself up on his arms so I could caress my clitoris.

'Come for me, Ariana,' he commanded, slowing the pace of his penetrations just enough for me to be able to obey him.

'Oh, yes, yes!' I gasped. 'I'm coming... I'm coming!' It was impossible, but it was true, I was climaxing faster than I ever had. His professional massage had relaxed my body so much it offered absolutely no resistance to the pleasure, and the orgasm that overwhelmed me just seemed to keep going and going beneath his deep hard strokes and there was no way I could control my cries, which I was vaguely aware were loud enough to be heard by his neighbors even through the walls and closed windows. Yet when I could focus again, he did not appear at all concerned I might get him kicked out of the building, in fact, he was smiling down at me approvingly.

'Now it's my turn,' he warned.

* * *

I had the dubious pleasure of showering in Gerald's bathroom. I was sticky with massage oil, and there was a good amount of cum on my breasts and belly since he had pulled out as he climaxed and ejaculated all over me. The man was a talented sculptor, he was smart and sensitive, but no one could call him a good housekeeper. His bathroom was not the cleanest I had ever bathed in, and I found myself aching to take his domestic affairs in hand along with his sexual ones. After our quick shower, we got dressed again to go out for dinner. A long massage and great sex had burned up the champagne and strawberries and I was starving. We lingered in his apartment, however, so I could have the pleasure of standing in the middle of the kitchen relishing the fact that it would soon be history. It would be great fun to design my own cooking space, and I couldn't wait.

'So, when is this all going to start happening, Gerald?' I couldn't resist asking.

He came up behind me and slipped his arms around my waist. 'As soon as we want it to start happening.' He kissed the top of my head as if to say I would have to change the way I thought about things living with him. My previous relationship had gotten me accustomed to thinking everything was difficult and required a great deal of time and effort, mostly on my part, but this was not, miraculously enough, going to be the case from now on with Gerald Loren.

I laid my head back against his shoulder. 'I feel so blessed,' I sighed.

'So do I,' he murmured, and dinner was further delayed by a long kiss and embrace beside the book-filled oven.

We had dinner at John Martin's that night and I enjoyed everything about it, yet the more we ate out the more I longed to start cooking again in earnest. We sat across from each other at a table on the balcony overlooking the bar, contentedly talking while we waited for the waitress to bring us our orders.

'I make a great red wine roast,' I told him.

He smiled at me as though I was a child he was very fond of. 'I'm sure you do.'

'So… so when can we fly up to Boston for my stuff?' I blurted.

'Tomorrow if you like,' he replied placidly.

'Tomorrow?' I laughed because he was never ceasing to amaze me.

'Although I suppose airfare would be cheaper if we bought it a few days in advance.'

'I already have my ticket; I bought a roundtrip down here. I wasn't expecting to meet my soul mate at the funeral, you know.'

'Always expect the unexpected. Who was it said that?'

'I have no idea.'

'What's the date on your ticket?'

'Next Wednesday.'

'Then why don't we fly up then?' he suggested. 'I can put my work into temporary storage.'

'Oh, God, I don't want anything to happen to it.'

'It'll be fine, the gallery can recommend a place for me, and the sooner we get your stuff down here, the better. It's great you can write from anywhere and don't have to worry about giving notice at some job up there.' He caressed my knee beneath the table, suddenly looking almost somber. 'You feel you're doing the right thing, don't you, Ariana? I'm not rushing you into anything, am I?'

'Gerald,' I grasped his hand fervently with both of mine, 'there isn't the slightest doubt in my mind or in my heart. I want to be with you more than anything.'

'I'm glad,' he whispered, staring so deeply into my eyes I could almost literally feel our souls touching, 'because I love you, Ariana.'

'I love you too, Gerald.'

CHAPTER FIFTEEN

I was planning a little dinner party. Rosa had invited Ernesto over and I had invited Gerald. It felt a little strange entertaining my mother's date at the same time as my own, but I quickly got over it and spent a good part of the day preparing for the important occasion of the two men in our lives meeting for the first time. I paid a visit to the grocery store in the morning and bought more ingredients than I needed because I still hadn't been able to decide what to prepare as the main course, which meant I also couldn't pick the appetizers yet. Thankfully, Gerald was in charge of the wine; he would be calling me later for the menu so he could select the appropriate grapes for each entrée. I was torn between formal and casual, low-fat and sinfully gourmet...

MY OLD CLOTHES

This is another traditional Cuban dish literally translated,

Ropa Vieja. Maybe it got it's name because of the shredded flank steak, that sort of evokes ragged clothing, and also because old clothes can be very comfortable and this is prime comfort food.

1 lb of Flank Steak
2 1/2 Cups Water
Sea Salt + Black Pepper
2 Tbls Extra Virgin Olive Oil
2-3 tsp minced Garlic
1/3 cup White Wine
1 can or jar of Sofrito
1 Bay Leaf
1 can sliced Potatoes, drained and well rinsed

Put the Flank Steak in a large shallow pan, pour the water over it, and bring to a gentle boil. Turn the heat down to medium-low, cover and simmer for one hour, turning the meat over once during cooking. Remove it from the pan and pour the broth into a cup.

Let the Flank Steak cool, and then shred it down the grain lengthwise into very thin strips. This takes some patience, but it's kind of fun, too. Season it well with Salt and Pepper.

Pour the Olive Oil in the pan and add the minced garlic, sautéing for a couple of minutes over medium heat. Turn the heat up to high and add the shredded Flank Steak. Brown the meat, stirring often, and then add the White Wine into the pan. Allow the Wine to evaporate somewhat before pouring the Sofrito over the meat. Stir well to mix and toss in the Bay Leaf. Bring to a boil, turn the heat down as low as possible, cover and cook for 30 minutes.

Add the sliced potatoes to the pan, stir to mix, cover again and cook another 45 – 60 minutes. Serve accompanied by White Rice and Cole Slaw.

YOGURT COLESLAW

1/3 head of Cabbage sliced into fine strips
Shredded Carrot
1/3 cup Organic Plain Yogurt
1/4 cup light Safflower Mayonnaise or your brand of choice
1 tsp Sea Salt
1 tsp Black Pepper
2 Tbls Red Wine Vinegar
2 tsp Lemon Juice
1 tsp Sugar

Combine the Yogurt with the Mayonnaise and seasonings, stir the mixture into shredded Cabbage and Carrots. Always serve chilled.

GOURMET GRITS

2 Cups Organic Chicken Broth
1 tsp Sea Salt
5 Tbls chopped green onions, white parts only
2 cloves Garlic, minced
2 1/2 cups Water
1 Cup Quick Grits

1/4 cup freshly grated Parmigiano-Reggiano Cheese

In a medium-sized saucepan, bring the Chicken Broth, Salt, Green Onions and Garlic to a slow boil, reduce the heat to low, cover and simmer for 5-10 minutes.

Turn the heat back up to high, pour in the 2 1/2 cups Water and bring to a boil. Slowly add the Grits, stirring, reduce the heat to medium-low and cook, continuing to stir often, until the Grits achieve a nice creamy consistency. At that point, remove the pan from the heat, add the grated Parmigiano-Reggiano Cheese and stir to melt it into the Grits. Serve at once. (If you use regular bottled Parmesan cheese, the results will not be quite as intensely flavorful and Risotto-like).

LADIES OF THE NIGHT SPAGHETTI

12 oz Spaghetti (cooked according to package directions)
2 Tbls Extra Virgin Olive Oil
3 tsp minced Garlic
1/2 cup Black Olives, chopped
1/2 cup oil-cured Black Olives, chopped
8 Anchovy fillets, minced
1/2 tsp Dried Oregano
1 28 oz can Crushed Tomatoes
2 Tbls Capers
Fresh Parsley, minced (approximately ? cup)
1/2 tsp Sea Salt
Freshly ground Black Pepper
Freshly grated Parmigiano-Reggiano Cheese

While you cook the Spaghetti, heat the Olive Oil over medium heat in a large saucepan and sauté the Garlic for about one minute before adding the Black Olives, the minced Anchovy and the dried Oregano. Cook for another sixty seconds, stirring most of the time, then add the crushed Tomatoes.

Turn the heat up to high and simmer the mixture, uncovered, for approximately five minutes, stirring once or twice, then add the Capers and the fresh Parsley, seasoning with the 1/2 tsp of Sea Salt and lots of freshly Ground Black Pepper. Serve at once over the hot Spaghetti and top generously with the freshly grated Parmigiano-Reggiano Cheese. This recipe makes enough for two generous main courses or four modest ones. This is my slight variation of a classic Italian dish that is not to be missed if you love Anchovies and fresh robust flavors having a shameless orgy on your tongue! A cool mixed green salad barely coated by a very light dressing makes a splendid accompaniment.

* * *

By early afternoon I had settled on the menu and, exhausted by my gourmet ponderings, I fell back across my bed and just lay there staring up at the blank white ceiling without seeing it, like a screen in a movie theatre playing out the colorful epic of all the thoughts and emotions rushing through me. It seemed a blessing beyond belief the man I had fallen so helplessly and completely in love with possessed more good qualities than even I would have dared to hope for. I kept thinking I should feel he was too good to be true, and yet how I really felt was that he was too good not to be true, which was perfectly in keeping with my positive view of life and the infinitely profound benevolence of the universe. If I had not truly believed and known in my heart such a man could exist, I would have settled for less; I had had plenty of opportunities to settle down in a relationship, but I had been incapable of doing so. Every love affair I had ever had came with a mysterious expiration date I did my best to ignore was there, but in the first moment of meeting a man, my soul somehow always knew he was not the person whose companionship could fulfill and sustain me for the rest of my life. What was vitally different about Gerald (apart from what an intelligent, talented, attractive, marvelous person he was) was that my soul could not find an expiration date on our relationship anywhere even though experience had taught me to perhaps be overly cautious and just a touch cynical despite my fairytale-like belief in true love. Not only was he an incredibly talented sculptor, he could apparently also build more mundane things with his hands, such as a brand new kitchen for me! I was discovering there really was such a thing as happily ever after, not in the sense of living trouble and worry free – that's impossible in the human condition – but in the sense that there's no reason whatsoever why you shouldn't try to make all your dreams and desires, big and small, come true every day for the rest of your life. I personally couldn't think of a better way to spend my time on earth, and now I had the partner with which to truly be able to put my philosophy into action every hour and every minute that remained to me of my hauntingly pleasurable and challenging incarnation.

'Ariana?'

'I'm in my room, mami.'

'Por Dios, how many things are you cooking at once? There's something burning!'

I sighed. 'There's nothing burning!' I yelled through my closed door. 'Just relax…'

'Ariana!'

'What?' I snapped, sitting up in annoyance.

'There's a police car in our driveway! Why is there a police car in our driveway?!'

I leapt out of bed and tried desperately to see between the foliage growing in front of my window. I could make out the black-and-white of a squad car parked out front, but that was all. 'It can't be,' I muttered, 'he's temporarily suspended from duty…' But my heart was beating so hard inside my rib cage I felt completely guilty about the way I had tried to avoid the inevitable. I should have known better than to try and blow a man like that off with an indifferent silence. I felt as though I was getting a speeding ticket from the Cosmos for going too fast sexually with a total stranger and then breaking the romantic speedometer altogether with my romance with Gerald.

'Good afternoon, officer,' I heard my mother say politely out in the foyer. 'Is there a problem?' Apparently she had opened the front door before he had time to ring the bell. 'What can I do for you?' she added anxiously, and I held my breath as I barely caught the sound of a deep male voice responding. 'Ariana?!' she practically gasped my name. 'She hasn't done anything wrong, has she?'

Thanks, mom. I glanced down at myself in dismay. I was wearing the gray shorts and T-shirt just threads away from disintegrating with black leather flip-flops, and I hadn't even bothered to comb my hair yet, but there was no avoiding it. I opened my bedroom door and flapped down the corridor.

Rosa gave me an anxious, wide-eyed look as I approached in which I caught just the slightest glint of suspicion. Poor mami, she would never know how bad I had been. I couldn't be sure yet the policeman actually was Eric since he was hidden behind the open door, but all my instincts already knew for certain what my brain could only guess. I wasn't, however, expecting the devastating effect the sight of him would have on my senses. I barely noticed her melting away as I said, 'It's okay mami, he's a friend of mine' because I wasn't really aware of anything except the black uniform and black boots which made the man inside them look as sexy and powerful as an embodiment of the universe itself. 'Hello, Eric,' I added automatically, my eyes finally making it up to his face after being helplessly trapped in the orbit of the dangerous objects hanging from his belt, one of which was obviously a gun.

'Hello, Ariana.' His light, wolf-like eyes seemed to sink into mine like fangs painfully challenging me not to desire him.

'Would you like to come in?' I asked, my mother's presence in the house making me feel relatively safe.

'No thank you,' he glanced over his shoulder at the squad car, 'I'm on duty.'

I got the impression he was showing off, which amused and annoyed me in equal measures. 'Yes, I see that. I thought you were suspended.'

'I was.'

'Well, I'm happy you're back on duty.'

'Thank you.'

I didn't bother asking him how he got my address or why he had come by; I imagined I knew the answer to both questions and there was nothing I could do about either one of them. He looked me up and down slowly, and I let him get his fill without volunteering anymore information about my love life. 'I'm sorry, I'm not dressed for company,' I said lightly.

'You look beautiful.' He subjected me to that penetrating stare again.

'You don't look so bad yourself,' I confessed.

'Are you still seeing someone?' He finally came bluntly to the point as his right hand came to rest on the holster of his gun, and he glanced back at the police car again. He had left the motor running.

'Yes, I am, Eric. We're flying up to Boston soon and driving a truck down with my things. We're moving in together.'

'Jesus, you sure don't waste any time.'

'Time is the fire in which we burn,' I quoted Delmore Schwartz blithely out of the blue.

'Are you sure you're not going to get burned rushing into a relationship like this?'

'I appreciate your concern, Eric,' and I really did, 'but I've never been more sure of anything in my life.'

'Well,' he took a step back, 'at least you'll be living here in Miami where I can catch you if you fall.'

I looked at him tenderly. 'That's very sweet of you, officer, but I'll be fine, really...'

He saluted me as he turned away. 'We'll see.'

His cynical attitude might have annoyed me if I hadn't felt blissfully beyond it. I closed the front door as he slipped back into the squad car. Then I reluctantly turned to face my mother, whose fists were placed firmly on her hips in a way that told me I was in for an interrogation.

'Gerald isn't involved in anything illegal, is he?'

'That was Eric, and he has nothing to do with Gerald.'

'Are you sure?'

'Yes, I'm sure!' I replied testily, and attempted to take refuge in the kitchen.

She followed me. 'You haven't answered my question, Ariana. Who was that man, and why was he here?'

'Remember I told you about the key to my rental car breaking in half? He's the locksmith who made me a new one. He was working with his uncle, or someone, while he was temporarily suspended from active duty. He's the man I met for drinks at the Colonnade the other night. I had sex with him twice and he didn't want to take no for an answer when I told him I was seeing someone else and it was very serious so I couldn't ever see him again.' I concentrated on stirring the sauce simmering on the stove.

'You had sex with him twice?' she asked faintly. 'But when…?'

'In the back of the locksmith's shop and in a phone booth at the Colonnade. I don't know why, but I just couldn't resist him, and if I hadn't met Gerald, I'm sure I'd be dating him right now. Me dating a cop, imagine that!'

Rosa crossed herself as if even the thought was too much to bear.

* * *

I should have known Gerald and Ernesto would get along as if they'd known each other forever. They were both straightforward, intelligent men with not a single deceitful poser's cell in their bodies, which was more refreshing to me than I can express. The wine and the conversation flowed freely and the food (if I don't say so myself) was delicious. It was dawning on me in a wonderful way how simply pleasurable and relaxing I found Gerald's company despite how powerfully attracted I was to him sexually and how passionately in love I was with him emotionally. I could be completely myself with him, in fact, I had been completely myself with him since we met and not even realized it. It was like living with a minor physical ache that's always been there and not noticing it's gone until you become aware that the much deeper tension it generated is no longer there and you're relaxed like you've never been before. Not being able to be completely myself in all my previous relationships with a man was a pain in my soul that had suddenly vanished. With every day Gerald and I spent together, I felt myself mysteriously unwinding, and as a consequence discovering just how much of my vital energy had been taken up worrying and being afraid I would never meet the right person. I felt intensely vital now, as though all of my mental and spiritual resources had been freed up so I could pursue my desires and goals with even greater skill and motivation. It's hard to describe, but I think what I was going through is what the proverbial poets are talking about when they say the world feels different – brighter and more beautiful – when you're in love, truly in love and not just blindly intoxicated by the novelty of a new relationship.

Since it was a pleasantly cool night, we all ended up outside on the back porch. Thanks to the high stone wall and the abundant jungle-like foliage, we felt completely private even surrounded by houses on three sides. Mami and I had pulled out all the stops for this special night (that's a curious expression I like very much pulling out all the stops… after all, why should your ever stop in the pursuit of happiness, a revolutionary concept penned by Jefferson implying there's much more to life than mere physical survival, but I digress…) which meant there were romantic oil lights strategically placed across the stone patio, and the wrought-iron chairs were all softened by colorful cushions, and Medieval lute music was drifting outside from the living room, imbuing the night with a rather surreal timeless quality since the Renaissance had happened in an entirely different climate.

Mami and Ernesto sat beside each other at the glass-top table across from Gerald and me. Both men had brought wine as an offering, and by then I think we were on our third bottle. The fervent chirping of crickets and cicadas complimented the softer, centuries-old string music in an interesting way I found both stimulating and relaxing, and I was drunk enough on love, intensified by the fruit-of-the- vine, to think Gerald's profile the most strikingly beautiful in all of male human history. He was listening to Ernesto with a soft, inscrutable smile on his lips I already loved more than anything. My mother's distinguished friend and lover was discussing the increasingly sorry state of affairs in Cuba, a subject I was all too familiar with even as I found the terrible living conditions there impossible to fathom. Here I was, a gourmet cook (at least in my own mind) hearing about people who more often than not eat boiled cabbage for dinner, employing ingenious methods to make it taste as much like meat as possible. I found the subject depressing, especially since there was absolutely nothing I could do about it, and Ernesto must have picked up on my intangibly growing restlessness because he changed the subject.

Our little gathering dispersed shortly afterwards (Ernesto had to be up early for work) and while mami walked him out to his car, I grasped Gerald's hand and play snuck him into my bedroom. We hugged fervently. The evening had been thoroughly enjoyable, but it had also been a torment not to be able to touch him and kiss him as much as I craved to.

'I should be going,' he said.

'Oh, no, not yet!' I wailed quietly, although I hardly blamed him for being turned off by a parental presence.

'It's been a long day,' he insisted gently but relentlessly. 'I worked on you for nine hours straight, and I have to say, you were exhausting.'

'I think I'm jealous of my clay alter ego,' I teased, keeping my arms wrapped possessively around his neck as I reached up to kiss his lips again.

'Don't be.' He pressed me against him. 'You're going to be the star of the show, Ariana Padron.'

CHAPTER SIXTEEN

I couldn't get enough of Gerald's cock. I was torn between gazing admiringly at his erection whenever it was in my hand towering before my face, and the hunger to fill my mouth with its gloriously warm, smooth and mysteriously flavorful dimensions, not to mention the desire to feel it thrusting up between my thighs and deep into my pussy. He obliged me by letting me lick and gaze, suck and swallow and stare, pump and fondle, for as long as I wanted to before granting my ultimate wish and stabbing the haunting wound between legs with his hard-on. His erect penis was straight as a column except for the slightest, sweetest bend in the center that just made it appear even more magnificent to me. And I absolutely loved the fact that he shaved the base of his cock as well as his balls, which made licking his scrotum a totally luscious experience for me. I thoroughly enjoyed bouncing his soft, heavy sack in the palm of my hand as my face slurped noisily over his shaft. At first I had felt somewhat self-conscious about making too much noise while I went down on him, but the soft, deep sounds of pleasure he made encouraged me to be as audibly greedy as I felt like being. Yet much as he obviously enjoyed my blow jobs, he rarely came in my mouth; he seemed to prefer the tight, clenching caress of my cunt and the way I deliberately milked his erection with my vaginal muscles.

I loved pleasuring him orally, but at first I was reluctant to let him do the same for me as often. In the past it had been very difficult, if not impossible, for me to climax into a man's mouth; it seemed my clitoris needed much more direct, even rough, stimulation. I should have known everything would be different with Gerald. I had believed how quickly I came the first time he went down on me was just a one-time blessing, and I was deliriously delighted to find myself proved wrong time and time again. My clit felt like a shy introvert exposed to a gentle yet relentless therapy, and I quickly came to realize I had been unnecessarily limiting myself. The problem wasn't my body's natural recalcitrance, the problem was it had never been the right head between my legs until now or the right hands and tongue and lips and knowledgably digging fingers. If he could work marvels with lifeless clay, it was nothing compared to what Gerald Loren could do with my malleable living flesh. He made me so wet when he was eating me it was a good thing he was a sculptor and kept plenty of spare towels lying around.

I spent two nights up in his apartment and didn't even bother going back to mami's house. I had all I needed right there, and at night we walked to whatever restaurant struck our fancy. I had brought over some select pieces of lingerie, and afternoon found me walking across the wooden floor in classic black high-heels and red stay-up stockings fondly caressing the slick black naked bodies surrounding me while Gerald watched me. Heels and stockings was all I was wearing, and for some reason they made me feel even sexier than just being completely naked. The extreme heels tilted my ass back, arched my spine and thrust my breasts forward, and the stockings clinging to my upper thighs made me even more enticingly aware of my tender sex lips and the vulnerable crack between them leading deep into my body. I wandered over to my clay altar ego. She was almost finished, and so lifelike I could almost feel the dreams she was having as she slept with her legs spread wantonly wide.

'Now walk back towards me,' my lover instructed from the other side of the room. 'Slowly,' he added.

I obeyed him gracefully, tossing my hair back away from my face as I held my head high.

'Beautiful,' he said, and when I was close enough to him, he grabbed one of my wrists impatiently. 'Bend over the table,' he commanded. 'I'm going to fuck you now.'

He meant the little glass table he had placed in front of the window so we could enjoy champagne and strawberries while watching the sunset. There were no blinds – the whole world could figuratively see my naked breasts bobbing wildly as he fucked me violently from behind, forcing me to cling to the edges of the glass and arch my back to take his beating. He was coming at me from an angle that made me feel as if his erection was rending me open around it; his penetrations almost hurt, yet I also perversely loved them. The experience was as strangely fulfilling for me as it was excruciating, and the possibility we were being watched slim as it was intensified my excitement. Yet I could only take so much, and he sensed this because he slipped out of me before coming. 'Come here,' he said gently, leading me into the bedroom and his wonderfully comfortable waterbed.

* * *

There you are!' my mother declared when I finally walked through the door again. 'Everyone wants to see you. Lourdes and Consuelo are meeting us at–'

'Mami, I'm exhausted, I can't see anyone today, okay?' I flung my back-pack down with a groan of relief.

'And what have you been doing for the last two days that you are so exhausted?'

'Fucking.'

'Ariana!'

'Well, you asked.'

'Would it really hurt you to spend some time with me and your two aunts this afternoon? They haven't seen you in ages.'

I groaned again as I sank down onto the couch. 'But they never stop talking!' I whined. 'And I just don't feel like dealing with people right now.' I leaned my head back against the cushions and closed my eyes. 'I have to call rental truck companies up in Boston, and my landlord is going to kill me for not giving him notice, and if I don't write an article soon I'm not going to have enough money to–'

'Fine, whatever,' she cut me off using the word I had driven her crazy with in high school. 'I'll probably see as much of you when you move down as I do now.'

I opened my eyes and turned my head to look at her where she still stood by the front door. 'That's not true, mami,' I assured her, because her forlorn stance made my heart contract guiltily. 'I'll go shower and change and spend the afternoon with you and Lourdes and Consuelo, okay? I just need to sit here for a few minutes.'

She cheered up at once, and came to perch on the couch beside me. 'What's this?' Smiling, she reached out to curiously touch the silver band around my neck.

'Gerald gave it to me,' I said languidly, closing my eyes again.

'It looks like an antique,' she observed. 'It's lovely... little silver roses...'

'Yes, it belonged to his great-grandmother,' I murmured. 'He said he's been waiting for the right woman to give it to.'

She rested her small, cool hand over my larger warm one. 'He's a real man,' she stated firmly. 'I'm so happy for you, Ari, finally!'

I opened my eyes and smiled at her. 'I'm happy for you, too, mami.' I sat up, suddenly curious. 'When did you and Ernesto... you know, when did you realize you felt more than friendship for each other?'

She shrugged. 'Oh, I don't know...' She looked away almost shyly. 'It just happened.'

I laughed. 'Well, that's specific.'

'It happened when I tripped on an escalator at Coco Walk and he caught me in his arms to keep me from falling!' she confessed abruptly in a single breath.

'What?' I laughed again. 'Tell me more!' I demanded.

'Well...' she stared into space, remembering. 'I was frightened, I could have seriously hurt myself, and it took me a moment to find my balance again, so I had to keep holding on to him, and then I looked up into his eyes...'

My own eyes watered sentimentally gazing at her expression. 'Oh, that's so beautiful,' I whispered mistily.

'We rode the whole way down just looking at each other. When we got off the escalator at the bottom, he let go of me finally, but he kept my hand in his, and even though we didn't say anything, even though we just kept walking, from that moment on we both knew...'

'Oh, mami.' I hugged her warmly.

'Ari, please, you don't know your own strength.'

'I love you, mami, and I'm so happy I'll be living close to you again. I can't believe I wasted so much time up in Boston.'

'Ay, si, Por Dios, I don't know what you were thinking.'

I stood up. 'I was thinking the scene down here in Miami was just too superficial and that the intelligent, sophisticated, profound man I was looking for was much more likely to be found up North in an old, cultured city full of universities.'

'And we don't have universities here? Please!' she scoffed. 'The first rule of true love,' she stated decisively as if she actually owned a copy of True Love For Dummies, 'is that your soul mate can be anywhere, and usually he's where you least expect him to be. And usually,' she followed me up, 'you find him when you least expect to, when you've learned to be happy on your own.'

I smiled. 'Like some cosmic reward?'

'Precisamente. Now go get dressed, Ari.'

'Yes, mami.'

* * *

I was forced to endure lunch with my mother and my two aunts. To tell the truth, it really wasn't all that bad; I rather enjoyed being the center of attention, and listening to Rosa describe Gerald in glowing adjectives gilded with phrases like 'Italian artist' 'Italian sculptor' 'smoldering Italian eyes' and so on, all delivered in Spanish, naturally, which made them sound even more romantically amusing to my English-speaking brain. The three sisters could not have been more different, but they all loved each other dearly so my mother's happiness for me was their happiness, and by the time we got

4

4

back to the house, my psyche was saturated with congratulations to the point where I almost felt mysteriously nauseous. I only had a sandwich for lunch (as I said, I prefer to eat and drink at night) but I still found it necessary (probably due to my exertions at Gerald's apartment earlier that morning more than to the food) to take a luscious cat-nap, during which I dreamed of sandwiches and the new dream-kitchen I would prepare them all in...

MY FAVORITE CHICKEN SANDWICH

3 boneless skinless Chicken Breasts
Extra Virgin Olive Oil
Garlic Olive Oil
Sea Salt
Freshly Ground Black Pepper
Powdered Thyme
Powdered Garlic
2 Sandwich-Sized Cuban Bread Loaves (or one large one cut in half)
Light Safflower Mayonnaise or Chipotle Mayonnaise
Extra Sharp Cheddar Cheese, sliced thick
1 Large Tomato, thickly sliced
Romaine Lettuce Leaves

Drizzle Extra Virgin Olive Oil over one side of the Chicken Breasts, rubbing it in with your fingertips, then season them generously with the Sea Salt, some freshly ground Black Pepper, a nice dusting of the powdered Thyme, and a moderate sprinkling of the Garlic Powder. Turn the Breasts over and repeat the process, only this time use Garlic Olive Oil and omit the Powdered Garlic. You can now refrigerate them for a few hours.

When you're ready to prepare the sandwiches, pre-heat the oven to 350° while heating a frying pan over high heat. When the pan is nice and hot, brown the Chicken Breasts on both sides for a few minutes, then place them in a shallow oven pan and bake them for 20 minutes. Turn them over and bake another 20 minutes or so, depending on how big and thick the Breasts are.

Meanwhile, slice the Cuban Bread* in half to make sandwiches and cover each half with some Light Safflower or Chiptole Mayonnaise. Now take a block of Extra Sharp Cheddar Cheese** and slice nice thick slices to lay across the bottom half of each sandwich.

When the chicken is almost done, pre-heat a large electric grill (or two small ones.)Carefully cut each breast in half lengthwise and cover the bottom half of each sandwich with as much breast meat as you can fit on it. Drizzle a bit of the juice from the roasting pan over the chicken, then top it with the Tomato slices and the Romaine Lettuce leaves. Place the top half of the bread over the lettuce and press down hard.

Grill the sandwiches until the bread is nice and crisp and the cheese has melted, remove them from the grill and cut them in half. (If you have any left over chicken breast meat, treat your pet to it or put it in your lunch salad the next day.)

*If you're not lucky enough to be able to find Cuban bread, use as light a French bread as you can find because you don't want a thick hard chewy crust here; you want the bread thin and crisp so the taste of it doesn't interfere with all the other flavors. The bread is not the star here, it's only the vehicle used to put these ingredients together in a devastatingly delicious way.

**I cannot stress enough the difference high quality cheese makes in recipes. Whatever you do, don't use Kraft cheddar or any other pre-grated cheese on this recipe; it just won't pack the same gourmet punch.

CUBAN STEAK SANDWICH

2 very thin 8 oz Beef Steaks
1 tsp Garlic, minced
Juice of 1 Lime
Sea Salt
Freshly ground Black Pepper
1 Tbls Extra Virgin Olive Oil
Light Safflower Mayonnaise
2 Sandwich-sized (approx 6 inches) Cuban Breads
4 Romaine Lettuce Leaves
Thin Tomato Slices
2 Tbls chopped Spanish Onion
2 Tbls fresh Parsley, minced

Season the Steaks with the minced Garlic, the Sea Salt and the Pepper, and fry them in the olive oil over high heat until cooked through; it won't take long if the steaks are nice and thin.
Cut the Cuban bread in half lengthwise, spread some mayonnaise on both sides, then on the bottom half lay the

Romaine Lettuce Leaves, cover them with the Tomato slices followed by the chopped Onion, the Parsley and the Steak. Place the top piece of bread over the steak and heat the sandwiches in an electric grill until the bread is nice and crisp and golden.

DEEP SOUTH CATFISH

2 Catfish Fillets (I use farm-raised) approximately 8 oz each
Sea Salt
Freshly ground Black Pepper
Cayenne Pepper
1/2 cup Corn Meal
1/4 cup Unbleached White Flour
1 Egg, beaten
Canola Oil for deep drying

Season the Cat Fish fillets with a modest amount of Sea Salt and freshly ground Black Pepper, then dust it with Cayenne Pepper (I only use about 1/8 of a tsp because I don't like my food too spicy).

Spread the Corn Meal out on one plate and the Flour out on another. Dredge the Cat Fish in the Flour, dip in the Beaten Egg mixture, then coat it with the Corn Meal. I like to repeat the process for an extra thick and crispy crust.

Heat the Canola oil over medium heat until hot, and fry the fillets for about fifteen minutes, turning once or twice. Serve with fresh Lemon wedges and some Tartar Sauce if you like. This is traditional Southern Fried Cat Fish and it's absolutely delicious.

CRISPY JUICY SKINLESS FRIED CHICKEN

4 very large (or 6 small) skinless Chicken Thighs (approximately 1 1/2 pounds)
Sea Salt
Freshly Ground Black Pepper
1 Egg (if it's small, use two)
1/4 Cup Soy Milk (or regular milk)
1/2 tsp Sea Salt
1 Cup Unbleached White Flour
1 tsp Sea Salt
Freshly Ground Black Pepper
Canola Oil for frying

Rinse the Chicken Thighs and season them with the Sea Salt and the freshly ground Black Pepper.

Beat the Egg in a shallow bowl and stir in the Soy Milk and 1/2 tsp Sea Salt.

On a large plate, spread out the Flour mixed with 1 tsp Sea Salt and some freshly ground Black Pepper.

Lightly coat the Chicken Thighs with flour, then drench them with the Egg and Soy Milk before thoroughly dredging them with more Flour, tossing it up over the Chicken with your fingertips if necessary. This is a messy procedure and you'll have to rinse your hands, because after you've done it once, you have to do it all over again! That's right, repeat the process, adding more flour to the plate if necessary.

Heat the Canola oil on high heat until it reaches 360°, turn the heat down to medium-low, wait a minute or two, and then add the Chicken. Cook the thighs for ten minutes on one side, turn them over and cook another ten minutes before beginning to test for doneness with an instant read meat thermometer. Yes, you'll need a hot oil thermometer and a meat thermometer if you want to get this right. Under no circumstances slice into the Chicken to see if it's cooked; it will ruin the whole beauty of this recipe which is how crispy the outside is and how succulently juicy the meat on the inside is thanks to its crusty armor, so that you won't even miss the fatty, unhealthy skin.

CHAPTER SEVENTEEN

I spent most of the following morning on the phone with rental truck companies up in Boston. Now that I had made the decision to stay in Miami, I had no desire to fly back up north, but I was not about to abandon all my precious possessions. One of my favorite Film Noir movies is *Laura*, and I always remember a line spoken by her aunt after Laura's supposed demise, 'She loved all her things so' because that's how I felt about my things. I love to shop at Thrift Stores and affordable antique markets, which feel like digging for treasure; it excites me not knowing what special aesthetic items are destined especially for me to find. I enjoy stores like Crate & Barrel and The Pottery Barn as much as anyone, but their homogenous, imaginatively pasteurized quality also bores me. I can't really afford quality antiques, but up in my North End apartment were handfuls of items I loved dearly, such as my

Japanese salt-and-pepper shakers in the form of two crouching black panthers with rhinestone eyes. I had never used them in the kitchen; they sat on the gas fireplace mantel, the sacred guardians of my living space. Now all my small treasures would have a new home, and they wouldn't just belong to me anymore. I knew Gerald would appreciate them, which would double my enjoyment of them. With his help I would get everything I needed to bring with me into one truck, and it wouldn't be necessary to hire movers, thank God (I don't weight lift for nothing.) It was tempting to fly up and then rent a truck the very next day, but the idea of spending a few nights up in Boston with my beautiful sculptor was also appealing. It all depended on him and how soon he had to get back in order to continue working on his scheduled one-man show at the gallery. The funny thing was, I didn't really have anyone I needed to say goodbye to up north except my brother, who I knew would be sorry to see me go. I had never much enjoyed hanging out with other women; all my friends and relationships had been with men, and they had all come to an end (sooner or later) leaving me alone again, which was how I liked it before I finally met Gerald. The call to my landlord had not been as unpleasant as I had feared it would be. Even though I was essentially only giving him a week's notice, there was a mile-long list of people waiting for a rent-control apartment in my neighborhood; he probably had it rented fives minutes after he got off the phone with me. Everything was pretty much set. Fortunately, Gerald had been able to book a seat on my same flight, and even though we might not be able to actually sit together, at least he would be soaring through the heavens with me.

In the afternoon I took a long hot shower to slough off the

tension of arranging to move all my stuff thousands of miles. I shaved my pussy and washed my hair and relished lathering myself up with my exfoliating sponge, lingering in the bathroom's sensual little temple as long as possible. I was exchanging a relentlessly cold climate for a relentlessly hot one, and the beauty of Spring and Fall for the paradisiacal monotony of constant greenery, but it didn't really matter. There are benefits and drawbacks to living anywhere, and all that truly mattered was being with Gerald. At least I could look forward to going around scantily attired in low-cut shirts exposing my cleavage and short skirts showing off my long legs.

I walked naked from the steamy bathroom into my cool bedroom, closing, then locking, the door behind me. I was suffering an irresistible urge to be naughty. I couldn't even remember how many orgasms I had enjoyed the two days and nights I spent at Gerald's place, but instead of being sated my body felt vibrantly alive and hungry for more pleasure. A good night's sleep had restored my energy, and I was more than ready to see him again this evening, but first I felt like indulging in a little appetizer by myself.

I lay back against the pillows on my bed, and just the sight of my erect nipples – long, rosy stamens jutting straight up out of the soft round hills of my breasts – was enough to turn me on. I spread my legs wide and arched my back so my beautiful tits rose before me and made me mysteriously hungry for my own body. My right hand was already between my legs fingering the deliciously smooth tenderness of my freshly shaved labia, two fingertips brushing lightly back and forth over my clitoris, which had proved was not as sleepy and stubborn to arouse as I had believed it to be. I had no problem whatsoever having an orgasm with Gerald in any position, which proved there was nothing wrong with my anatomy; I simply had not had the right partner, and therefore the right stimulation, until now.

I loved how my breasts looked – round, lush blooms pale as moons rising over the light-golden skin of my chest. My whole body was already lightly tanned except for my breasts and my sex, which made them look and feel even more temptingly vulnerable. I gasped with delight; my clitoris felt electric. It seemed just the slightest touch was enough to set it off and ignite my veins like fuses all explosively converging between my legs. I thrust my bosom up towards the ceiling, arching my back even more as the power of desire lifted me up like a disembodied force possessing my body even as I imagined Gerald's stiff cock penetrating me. I visualized his erection thrusting up inside me, and the pleasure I felt as I energetically stroked myself was almost overwhelming. I was already coming and yet I didn't want to, not yet. I wanted to prolong the ecstasy, to savor the molten bliss poured into the empty crucible of my sex forging an ecstasy as sharp and as fatally irresistible as a divine sword slicing up through my flesh. It was no use, in a matter of moments I was climaxing, my hips writhing against the comforter as I bit my lip in order not to cry out too loudly.

Afterwards, I felt sated and profoundly languid, so much so it was a while before I was able to make myself get up and start dressing.

* * *

I opened the door leading into Gerald's building and nearly collided with a woman who had obviously run down the stairs. I only got a brief glimpse of her lovely face, but it was all I needed to know her headlong flight had been prompted by intense emotions, none of them good. By contrast I felt as lighthearted and deeply content as a feather drifted off my guardian angel's wing as I ascended the steps to my lover's door. I raised my fist to knock politely, but a strange impulse made me test the knob first, and it turned in my hand. The door was unlocked, so I let myself in, subconsciously asserting my right to do so by virtue of our sexual and spiritual intimacy. I felt it was time there weren't any locked doors between us, in any sense. His back was to me as I entered. He was working on my clay body wearing a full-length white apron tied over s short-sleeved black t-shirt and the black jeans he looked so good in.

'Please leave,' he said coldly without looking over at me.

The door slipped out of my suddenly nerveless grasp and clicked shut behind me. I took a few steps towards him in my high-heeled sandals, too stunned to speak.

'It's over, can't you understand that?' His voice was hard as he angrily wiped his hands on his apron.

'Gerald?' I said, feeling as though I was about to faint and if he didn't catch me I would not survive the fall.

He looked over his shoulder. 'Ariana...' He strode towards me as though sensing he needed to reach me as quickly as possible, removing his dirty apron on the way. 'I thought... I didn't know it was you.' He dropped the clay-covered white cloth and took me in his arms, pressing me so hard against him I was scarcely able to catch my breath. But at least my heart had started beating again – the dead universe I had caught a horrifying glimpse of was gone and I was back in the wonderful world created by the horizon of his loving arms. He let go of me, and gazed down into my eyes with a look of concern. 'I'm sorry,' he repeated in the face of my shell-shocked silence.

'I saw a woman running out of the building.' I finally found my voice. 'Was she…?'

'Yes. I thought she had come back.'

'You only just now broke up with her?' I pitied her more than I could express, but I was also profoundly hurt to think he had still been involved with someone after all we had said to each other, not to mention done together.

'No, I told her it was over the day after I met you, but I don't think she believed me.' He stared steadily down into my eyes as he spoke so the truth of what he was saying penetrated directly into my soul, bypassing my suspicious brain. 'She kept calling even though I made it perfectly clear I didn't want to see her again, and today she just showed up. I'm sorry.'

'So am I, sorry for her. I can't even imagine how terrible it must be to lose you.'

He pressed my cheek against his chest, holding me tenderly against him now. 'You're so sweet,' he murmured.

'She was beautiful,' I remarked cattily, because mingled with my pity for her was also a fierce sense of triumph.

'Nowhere near as beautiful as you, Ariana.'

'Hmm.'

'What?' He held me at arm's length again. 'You don't believe me?'

I thought of the girl's long slender limbs and flowing reddish-blonde hair. 'She's beautiful, too,' I pointed out jealously.

'Yes, but not all the way through like you. No woman will ever be as beautiful to me as you are, Ariana, surely you realize that.'

'Yes!' I sighed, wrapping my arms hungrily around his chest

and closing my eyes as I rested my cheek against his warm strength. This is where I belong, I thought listening to his heart beating. He's all mine, all mine, all mine...

'I love you,' he whispered into my hair.

'I love you, too,' I whispered back, 'more than anything!'

* * *

That night we drove to South Beach and had dinner on Lincoln Road. It was fun strolling up and down the popular Avenue people watching (and dog watching, too, since many of the pedestrians were walking their prize pets) and idly window shopping while discussing the serious matter of what restaurant to honor with our patronage. We stopped for a drink at one place and ate at another, but the highlight of the evening was the chocolate gelato we had for dessert. Pleasantly sated, we walked back to my rental car. I had given Gerald the key forged for me by Eric, the Viking cop (as I would forever think of him) and he drove us safely back into Coral Gables and his apartment, where we would be spending the night.

My lover's spacious studio was dark when we entered, and our laughter sounded uncannily loud and alive in the silence looming with figures darker than the night around them. I was going to miss living surrounded by statues forever engaged in the art of lovemaking, but on the other hand it was going to be nice having all this space to work with. I was tipsy from good food and wine – not to mention from the intoxicating pleasure I always took in Gerald's company – so when he abruptly stripped off my shirt, I giggled happily. Ever since arriving in Miami, I had indulged in the pleasure of not wearing a bra, and I loved how pale and lovely my breasts looked in the darkness as he cupped them possessively in his slightly rough hands, then sucked hungrily on my nipples, moving back and forth between them in a way that was soon driving me crazy with desire. There was a direct connection between my nipples and my sex because the more he licked and sucked and gently bit my tit's stiff peaks, the warmer and wetter and needier my pussy got. The darkness was alleviated only by the light of a lamp on the street below, its bright yellow glow enchantingly diffused by the tree tops. It was just enough light to be able to make out each other's naked bodies as we impatiently stripped off all our clothes. He kicked off his leather sandals, but I kept my heels on. I knew he loved the way I looked in them and I also liked how much sexier they made me feel.

'Come here,' he said in a conspiratorial whisper, and led me over to the large black figure of a fully erect muscular man on his knees. There was the intimation of a woman's body pressed up against him from behind, her arms wrapped around his neck. He was bent forward slightly as if supporting her and her amorphous figure flowed behind him like a cape evoking a sense of his power as well as the weight of a burden. It was an interesting piece, but I had to admit the dimensions of the stone phallus appealed to me on a purely physical level. The straight, ribbed, eternally hard cock was almost obscenely large and a shiny, slick black even in broad daylight. It was impossible for me not to have naughty thoughts about that god-like hard-on every time I saw it, so I suffered a nervous stab of excitement when Gerald led me right to it.

'I've seen you eyeing this big black dick,' he said, and as always it thrilled me when he talked dirty. 'I want you to suck it, Ariana. I want you to suck that big black cock while I fuck you.'

'What?' I laughed, incredulous and yet also hopelessly turned on.

'You heard me.' He positioned me facing the breathtakingly well-hung figure kneeling on a pedestal that put his erection on a level with my breasts. All I had to do was bend forward at the waist to take it into my mouth, which is just what I found myself doing without protest as Gerald grabbed my hips and pulled them back against him, forcing me to brace myself on the muscular thighs of one of his creations. I thought about protesting, about complaining that it was no fun putting something cold and lifeless in my mouth, but for some reason I didn't. It didn't matter that the penis sliding between my lips and onto my tongue wasn't real since the one thrusting into my slick pussy from behind definitely was and the pleasure it filled me with was intense, stoking the darkly irresistible excitement I suffered at being filled up at both ends at once. I moaned as the cold, unyielding head grazed my tender throat, yet I was perversely compelled to take the lifeless dick all the way into my mouth. I was seduced by the fulfillment I experienced absorbing the full benefit of my lover's arousal as he observed my oral skills. I could feel his excitement deepening and his cock swelling as he watched my head bobbing back and forth, and I imagined he was remembering the feel of my mouth and throat even as he enjoyed the clinging caress of my pussy at the same time.

'Mm, yes, suck it!' he commanded breathlessly. 'I love watching you suck cock, Ariana.'

I moaned again from the effort, and from the escalating ecstasy of his penetrations, but then he pulled out of me abruptly. 'Turn around,' he ordered.

I obeyed him weakly, scarcely daring to realize what he had in mind even as part of me lusted after the sensual challenge.

'That's right, you can do it,' he encouraged me in a sexy voice I couldn't resist. 'I want you to fuck yourself with that big black cock while you suck me off... that's it...'

'Oh, my God!' I gasped, 'I can't... I can't... please...'

'Yes, you can,' he insisted quietly. 'You can, and you want to, and you're going to.'

There was no way my body could argue with his tone or with my own wild hunger. I cried out as I felt the bulbous stone head lodge itself in the entrance to my sex, but I couldn't resist pushing myself back against it. The statue's dick was slick with my saliva and my cunt was creaming helplessly, providing enough lubrication for the overwhelming penetration. I couldn't believe it, but I was willingly struggling to wrap my tight pussy around that massive rod. I wasn't satisfied to feel it only partially filling me. I wanted the full rending black length in my belly. I longed to feel the unyielding stone stuffing and impaling me. Then the sensation of Gerald's contrastingly tender hard-on slipping into my mouth intensified my fulfillment to such a critical point I started coming around the kneeling black man's eternal erection as my living lover fucked my mouth, his hips pumping selfishly in my face. I was stretched so completely open, so utterly fulfilled at both ends, that coming felt like being killed by my own wicked soul willing to sacrifice its flesh envelope for the sake of absolute pleasure. The orgasm I gave myself with that statue was so violent I was scarcely aware of Gerald's cum spurting down my throat, the sensation simply part of the whole blindingly transcendent experience.

'Very good, Ariana,' he said to me afterwards, yet I scarcely remember him lifting me up in his arms and laying me across his waterbed I was so sensually worn out and thought-lessly fulfilled.

CHAPTER EIGHTEEN

The next day there was no way in hell I could get out of spending time with my relatives. Gerald kindly offered to accompany me on my official familial rounds, doubly inescapable today that the news of my engagement and return to Miami had spread to even the most distant branches of the family tree. Like leaves blown in by the wind of gossip, dozens of Padrons were converging on Coral Gables to see me. I was tempted to accept my lover's kind offer, but resisted. I would only feel guilty about putting him through such a boring ordeal, which would make it even harder for me to endure. I would be happier thinking of him working in his studio while I suffered through one thoroughly loving interrogation after another. 'You'll have to meet some of my relatives eventually,' I told him, 'but not today.'

He kissed my forehead, and caressed the hair away from my face. 'I'd be happy to come,' he insisted.

'I know, but I'd rather you stayed here and worked.'

'I do have a lot of work to do before my show...'

'Yes, you do.' I found the strength to untangle my limbs and my emotions from around him for the moment as I walked determinedly towards the door. 'I'll call you when I get home,' I promised, then hesitated, my heart perching uncertainly on his smile. 'Um, you don't think... you're not expecting anymore ex-girlfriends to drop in and try to get back together with you, are you?'

He looked up at the ceiling. 'Hmm, let's see...'

'Gerald!'

He laughed, but said seriously, 'No, I'm not. Go have fun with your family.'

'Right!'

* * *

By the time mami and I pulled back into her driveway that evening my head was spinning. At first it had been fun being the center of attention, but then I had begun to feel rather like Prometheus – everyone wanted to know all there was to know about my new flame so they kept prodding me with questions and sometimes (in the case of certain female relatives) they even took little jealous, cynical pecks at me and my fairytale happiness. Whereas fucking Gerald for hours left me feeling physically worn out but otherwise profoundly invigorated, spending the day with relatives was utterly exhausting. I do not put great store in blood ties. In my opinion love and affection are the only valid links between people, and so because it meant so much to my mother (and especially to my grandfather) I spent the day feeling rather like Spartacus tied to the family tree – I had freed myself of all this only to be caught in the end because I had fallen in love with a Miami resident. God has a perverse sense of humor, indeed.

'Why did you need to keep that rental car all this time?' Mami asked me irritably as she parked beside it, and I could tell she was just as wrung dry by the day as I was whether she admitted it or not.

'Because I felt like it,' I snapped.

'You felt like wasting money when you have a perfectly good car right here?' she snapped right back.

'You're always using it, and I got a really good deal. I'm taking a shower now.' I got to the front door before she did and gratefully let myself into the blessedly cold house. Good central air-conditioning is an absolute imperative in Miami.

I still wasn't feeling quite like myself even after a long, hot beating beneath the fierce showerhead. I felt curiously cut up, as though my thoughts and feelings were hanging like bloody rags from my soul. Looking back on the day, my relatives struck me as a pack of hungry dogs, and many of them had been intent on mauling my happiness even while hypocritically pretending to be overjoyed by it. Human nature can be dark and depressing, especially when it's related to you and you're forced to get defenselessly nearer to it than you normally would. Of course, there were some Padrons I genuinely liked, and it had been nice seeing them again, but the overall effect of the family gathering had been to completely drain me. It was depressing how few people seemed to truly find their soul mates in this life, and as I dialed Gerald's number on my cell phone, I was amazed, and infinitely grateful, to know he was really there on the other end, and that any second now I would hear his voice, which already was more beloved to me than any other voice on this earth.

'Hello?' he answered briskly.

'I love you.'

His tone changed completely. 'I love you too, dear. Are you all right?'

'I think I'll live.'

'Good, then I'll swing by in about an hour and we'll go get you a drink.'

'Oh, yes, please!'

* * *

The instant Gerald and I were in each other's orbit, I felt whole again. The universe came into full glorious focus in his face, and the look in his eyes instantly massaged away all the tensions of the day. His company, enhanced by a glass of Chardonnay, was all I needed to become inspired, and we ended up staying home. I had spent half the afternoon in a restaurant surrounded by raucous relatives; I was craving the peace, quiet and solitary comfort of mami's living room. She was out with Ernesto for the evening, so my lover and I had the house all to ourselves again for a while.

'I'm making us soup and salad for dinner,' I announced.

'That sounds wonderful, but are you sure you wouldn't rather go out? I know you've had a hard day.'

'Mm, I wish I'd had a hard day…' I caressed his crotch through his jeans.

'You pleased me very much last night,' he said suddenly, holding me close where we sat together on the couch watching television with the volume turned almost all the way down while we talked.

'I can't believe you made me do that,' I murmured shyly.

'I didn't make you do anything,' he pointed out quietly.

'No, you're right, but you wanted me to…'

'And that's why you did it, Ariana, only because I wanted you to?'

'Well... no, I guess part of me wanted to do it, but... but mainly it was exciting for me because I knew I was pleasing you.'

His arm tightened around my shoulders. 'And that's just as it should be.'

'I think I would do anything you asked me to,' I dared confess to him, and to myself, at the same time.

'You think?'

I glanced up at his face. He was smiling softly down at me, but his eyes were serious. 'I know I would,' I corrected myself, resting my cheek on his chest. Wherever I was in the world, I would feel at home resting in his arms with my head against his chest.

'That's good, because you're mine, Ariana, all mine, now and forever.'

'Amen,' I sighed.

* * *

The next day passed like a dream of fulfillment too rich to remember the way looking too closely at the sun half blinds you, and that night Gerald and I crowned our glorious self-indulgence in all the conceivable pleasures of the senses by driving down to Kendall to feast on two-for-one Maine lobsters at Captain's Tavern. For over twenty-five years this bastion of seafood had been shipping hundreds of hapless crustaceans down from Maine every week to satisfy the lobster lust of patrons such as Gerald and me. I thought of my Vegan brother, and felt just a little sick to my soul picturing crates of doomed lobsters being carted into the bowels of the restaurant's hidden kitchen. I wondered how I would feel if advanced and gastronomically greedy aliens from outer space treated spaceships of humans in the same way. How would I like having my limbs snapped open on a dining table and the marrow sucked from my bones? I wouldn't like it at all, of course, but my lust for lobster was just too great to allow me to entertain such thoughts for more than a few guilty seconds in the face of the succulent white meat decadently dipped in butter at my fingertips. That night, Gerald and I were shameless contributors to the environmentally damaging excesses of civilization, and we loved every sinfully delicious second. We accompanied the Lobster with a dry and crisp Sauvignon Blanc, and even the loaded baked potato was good (although not as good as mine, Gerald was astute enough to point out.)

Afterwards, he was behind the wheel of my rental car again (we preferred its air-conditioned comfort to the less cushy interior of his Jeep) and we were driving back to Coral Gables. That afternoon I had packed a small suitcase, and everything I needed for our journey up to Boston tomorrow was at his place. I had already said a temporary goodbye to mami, who had cried not because I was leaving but because she was so happy I was coming back. Everything was set; in less than a week's time (if all went well) my possessions would be here in Miami and Gerald and I would be living together. My soul almost felt mysteriously sick I was so fulfilled.

When we entered his apartment, our arms around each other, the moon was shining directly down on the forest of statues, one of whom I had been wickedly intimate with, a fact that made the sensual figures seem more alive than ever. I hoped my flesh-and-blood lover didn't have anything similarly wild planned for tonight. I was tired, and just a little stressed out thinking about the plane flight tomorrow, not to mention the effort of loading a truck, then the long drive back down to Florida. I was glad that, after we both used the bathroom and brushed our teeth, all Gerald told me to do was take off my clothes before he lifted me up in his arms and laid me across his bed, in which I felt as safe and happy as a little girl whose dreams kept coming true as he lay down beside me and took me in his arms.

'Do you know how good, how right, you feel lying here in my arms like this?' he asked me gently.

'Yes…' My eyes were closed and I was already drifting off on a deep, sweet current of contentment.

'Do you have any idea how happy you make me?'

'As happy as you make me, I hope,' I murmured sleepily.

'Do you have any idea how much I love you?'

'And do you have any idea how long it's taken me to feel this way about a man and even about my own body… no man has ever made me appreciate myself the way you're helping me to. No man has ever made me feel so beautiful… I want to keep feeling this way forever… at least for a long, long time…'

'And why wouldn't you?'

'As long as I'm blessed like I am now, I will.'

'I'll always love you, Ariana, no matter what.'

'Then I'll always be blessed,' I said, drifting off into dreams that finally paled in comparison to the wonder of my waking life and love for Gerald.

RECIPE INDEX
(Chronological)

Magic Carpet Books

Maria Isabel Pita

The Story Of M…A Memoir	0-9726339-5-2
Dreams Of Anubis	0-9726339-3-6
Pleasures Unknown	0-9726339-6-0
Recipe For Romance	0-9726339-8-7

Marilyn Jaye Lewis

In The Secret Hours	0-9726339-4-4
When Hearts Collide	0-9726339-1-X
When The Night Stood Still	0-9726339-7-9

Alison Tyler

Blue Valentine	0-9726339-0-1
The ESP Affair	0-937609-45-5

Shauna Silverton

That Certain Someone	0-937609-46-3

Lucy Niles

The Engagement	0-9726339-2-8

Laura Weston

Dreams & Desires	0-937609-35-8